Not Long Ago Persons Found

Not Long Ago Persons Found

J. Richard Osborn

Bellevue Literary Press
NEW YORK

First published in the United States in 2025
by Bellevue Literary Press, New York

For information, contact:
Bellevue Literary Press
90 Broad Street
Suite 2100
New York, NY 10004
www.blpress.org

© 2025 by J. Richard Osborn

This is a work of fiction. Characters, organizations, events, and places (even those that are actual) are either products of the author's imagination or are used fictitiously.

Cover photographs by Ray Wise/Getty Images & NayaDadara/Shutterstock.com

Library of Congress Cataloging-in-Publication Data
Names: Osborn, J. Richard, author.
Title: Not long ago persons found / J. Richard Osborn.
Description: First edition. | New York : Bellevue Literary Press, 2025.
Identifiers: LCCN 2024059752 | ISBN 9781954276406 paperback acid-free paper
 | ISBN 9781954276413 epub
Subjects: LCGFT: Novels | Fiction
Classification: LCC PS3565.S377 N68 2025 | DDC 813/.54--dc23/eng/20250211

All rights reserved. No part of this publication may be reproduced or transmitted in any form or by any means, electronic or mechanical, including photocopy, recording, or any information storage and retrieval system now known or to be invented, without permission in writing from the publisher, except by a reviewer who wishes to quote brief passages in connection with a print, online, or broadcast review. No part of this book may be used or reproduced in any manner for the purpose of training artificial intelligence technologies or systems.

Bellevue Literary Press would like to thank all its generous donors—individuals and foundations—for their support.

 This publication is made possible by the New York State Council on the Arts with the support of the Office of the Governor and the New York State Legislature.

Book design and composition by Mulberry Tree Press, Inc.

Bellevue Literary Press is committed to ecological stewardship in our book production practices, working to reduce our impact on the natural environment.

♾ This book is printed on acid-free paper.

Manufactured in the United States of America.

First Edition

10 9 8 7 6 5 4 3 2 1

paperback ISBN: 978-1-954276-40-6
ebook ISBN: 978-1-954276-41-3

For the real Adam

Not Long Ago Persons Found

A VIOLENT COUNTRY

THE RIVER

We were on our way to the airport, a long ride. What had we done, what were our priors?

We'd driven the principal road in from the coast, through the small towns and settlements and marketplaces along it. And always from that road, between towns, between the buildings in the towns, there were views of the river. Between the shade cloths of the market squares, between the people, there were views of the river. On the paths we took down its banks were marks and deposits from the river at different stages of flood. At water level, wind flowed up the valley from the ocean, or sometimes it went the opposite way, the air, either way, shaped by the same curves as the river, the air carrying pollen and light seeds and insects, the river carrying heavier seeds and fish and their eggs and more other forms of life than we could see on land. Above, birds of prey lifted, circled, scanning the ground below for small animals going down to the water to drink.

In one place, we observed as a woman with a child on

her back went down to the river's edge and washed her feet. In another place, a large flock of small birds lofted suddenly from trees on the bank, an undulating, reshaping swarm of birds, black, then white, then black as they turned their backs or chests toward us. The cloud of them lengthened, curved, burst, then blobbed together densely again as they circled right above our heads, wings whirring, then landed in other trees, across the water, on the opposite bank. Which caused us to notice one hunting bird perched on the lone high branch of a denuded dead tree over there, looking at us as if—if we wanted to believe it—as if the bird recognized us after a long absence, as if we'd been there before, as if we belonged there. And then I noticed the sound of the river's current, steady and quiet, the flow of water and minerals and sloughed-off animal dreams being carried down to the ocean.

In that place, like some others, we broke off a tree branch, stripped it of leaves and twigs, attached an empty lab jar to the branch's narrow end, then pushed the jar up and held it aloft for a few minutes as merchants watched from the bank above. Then we brought the jar down, empty as far as anybody could see, tightened a lid onto it, applied a carefully filled-out label to it, and added it to our samples case.

As far as anybody in either government knew, that's what we were there to do, to take samples, and that is one thing we did. Samples of air, samples of plants that were sources of pollen in the air: samples from grasses and ferns and bushes, from tree-seed cones on the ground, from flowers up on trees that we reached with borrowed ladders—all possible sources of the pollen found in the boy's lungs, in his stomach, on his clothes. Pollen he could have acquired from breathing, from eating, from walking around.

We took samples of rocks and soils and rainwater to test as sources for the minerals in the boy's bones. But since what mattered wasn't minerals as they lay about, but minerals as taken up and deposited in the skeleton of an advanced organism, we also needed samples of actual bones, bones made locally, with the minerals of a specific place.

Human bones were available, black market, but a human—however it happened that their bones ended up for sale, illegally—that person, while alive, might have moved around some, as people do, so their bones would have taken up minerals from different environments, and so their bone-minerals profile wouldn't be representative of the minerals in bones from a single place. And we needed single-place bones if we were going to use them, by comparison, to locate the origins of the boy's bones.

As proxies for human bones, we had to go for bones attainable from local animals—parts and whole, some dead, some alive—fresh in market squares.

Live chickens were plentiful, ready for slaughter, but chickens are a universal currency, easily transported from place to place before their final end, so chicken bones would be of uncertain provenance. Also not bones from the live exotic birds and lizards and cats on offer, most also illegally, as any of those animals could have been smuggled a long distance in pursuit of the highest price.

To get bones reliably local, we bought recognizable parts of butchered goats or pigs, whole wild field rats, and the like. These we had boiled for us until the meat could be pulled off and given away, a few of the bones slipped into plastic bags, and the bags packed into the main compartment of our samples trunk, our rolling reliquary, the trunk that we believed was accumulating the objective truth about where the boy was from, the trunk that substantiated our faith that we could one day know why the boy left that place, and died so far from home.

At one bend in the river, where we had turned off the road and gone down to the water's edge and were taking air samples, my wife asked me if I could live there. She continued working, the look on her face the somber scientist, absorbed in details, far from me, as she often was. Could I live there, she repeated, not that exact location but . . .

"You ask that question everywhere we go," I said.

"And your answer here?"

"With you, yes," I said.

It rained. Observers on the bank above us retreated to shelter. We let ourselves get wet. Blood on the ground under carcasses in the market began to pool, dilute, and trickle down to the river, together with loose soil, motor oil, flecks of plant and animal decay from high and low in the watershed. The river muddied and began to rise, the whole cycle starting all over again.

If we looked up from the river, from the banks at water level, or from between the stalls and buildings of the marketplaces and towns along the river, we could see terraces, higher in the valley, above the settlements. Up there, evidence of a different sort lay.

HEADQUARTERS

'The body of a boy of about seven was found floating in the river in our city. The cause of death could have been a couple of things—'

"Drowned," the interrogator interjected, looking up from reading my statement back to me.

"Drowned maybe," I reminded him.

"Ha, maybe drowned," he repeated; then he resumed reading.

"'. . . the cause of death *could* have been a couple of things. The body couldn't be identified. He wasn't a missing person. Nobody was looking for him. An autopsy discovered pollen in his lungs from another place entirely—pollen from grasses and trees of what had to be a warm green valley around a different river, somewhere far from our city—a place the victim must have been not long before he died. The investigators, when they heard this, were stricken—were *stricken*—with a sense of incomparable melancholy. This boy, though in our city, had been carrying in him the other river, the fertile valley, a foreign sun. Then the sun was extinguished.'"

My interrogator stopped reading again and said,

"Memory of home. When he lost it, he . . . expired. Your city killed him."

I didn't reply.

"Hmm?" he prompted. Still nothing. He returned to my statement.

"'My wife'—your wife—'is a biological anthropologist, a forensic anthropologist; I am'—you are—'her assistant. We were sent to this country because our police believe that the valley around your principal river here could be where the boy came from.'"

"Upriver," my interrogator asserted, brushing something from his uniform that I couldn't see.

"Probably," I confirmed. He resumed.

"'One of our tasks'—your tasks—'was to collect samples of pollen locally, to compare to the pollen in the boy's lungs, to corroborate that this *was* the river, the valley— that he'd been in this vicinity for some time before he traveled. We could also use pollen to try to narrow it down, to try to identify a specific town or village that might have been his home.'"

"Okay, that's those samples. And the rocks and bones and pictures?" he asked.

"It's in there," I said. I pointed to my statement.

He sighed and went back to it.

"'The photographs we have are of the victim, as best we could. These photographs were to show around, to ask if anybody had seen this boy or knew his parents or any relatives.'"

My interrogator looked up again.

"You did find his family," he said.

"As I told you, no."

"You found people who knew his family."

"As I told you, no."

"Where does his family live?"

"We didn't find his family."

"You say."

My wife, in that interval, was in a separate room—I assumed answering the same questions as I was and making her own statement. I assumed calculating the same as I was what to leave out.

My interrogator read on.

"'Why we have rocks and dirt and animal bones in our luggage: to assay their mineral content, to trace to the minerals in the boy's bones—'"

"Ha. Radioactive," the interrogator interrupted himself again, skipping ahead.

"Isotopes. Everybody's bones have some," I said. "But the mix is different—"

"Depending on where you've lived," he filled in. "You think our rocks are in his bones."

"That's the hypothesis. I put all that in the statement," I said.

"Yes, and as to the bones, what did you do to his body?"

"Well, it was already . . ." I started, but stopped.

"You took samples from the bones in his leg? His arm?"

"Just fragments."

"You sawed a hole in him."

"Yes."

"That's not in here," he said, flapping the statement in my face.

"But the logic, the reason—"

"Ha. Okay. Moving on."

He looked for his place in my text again. "Dada dada dada da . . . right. 'So the pollen tells us where he'd been recently, and the bone minerals tell us his origin, where his bones were made. And then, even if we don't find his family now, even if we still don't know his name, at least the police can start for sure with his geography, where he's from. And then try to understand what caused the boy to leave his home and die in our city, pollen from the air of the faraway place still in his lungs.'

"The end," my interrogator concluded. "So, 'biological anthropologist,'" he noted, from earlier in the statement. "'Forensic anthropologist.' Secrets of the dead."

"Yes, that's it."

"Maybe death is not so mysterious."

He smiled, pleased with himself. He lifted the pages of my statement from the desk, turned toward the door, turned back, picked up the ballpoint pen I'd been using, replaced the cap, put the pen in his pocket.

"I think we need to work on you two some more," he said; then he left the room.

I looked up at the TV monitor hanging from a bracket in an upper corner of the room. On the screen was a funeral, a military funeral.

After some time, a different officer came into the room. He dropped my statement onto the desk without looking at it, sat down, and said, "Let's go over this again."

"You're the third," I said.

"No, I'm the first," he said, pointing to the patch on his shoulder, his patch green and gold, like the others, but with more stripes on it.

"You were here to gather samples of air, samples of plants, of bones—pigs and goats from the marketplace. You were here to ask questions. All related to an investigation of a death in your city."

"It's in my statement."

"And what else?"

"Nothing else."

"It was our river that was of particular interest."

"Yes," I said. "The river, the river valley, the watershed."

"Not the hills above."

"We did go up into the hills, to get the broad view."

"Particular hills, particular sites," he said.

"Locations with a view, to get a perspective," I said.

"And what did you see?"

"A verdant river valley, a variety of trees and plants. Not much wildlife."

The officer stood up, sat back down, leaned forward, lowered his voice.

"We are a sovereign nation," he said. "Not a whore whose clothes you can remove because you have paid."

"We had approvals. To investigate. Approvals at the highest levels. Your superiors."

"Ah, our superiors." He leaned back, as if to relax. "Our su-pe-ri-ors," he repeated, fitting his mouth precisely around the syllables. "Roof rats. It is their job to smile when you people expect it. It is our job, at this level, to maintain order." He paused for a significant stare at me. Then: "The body they found, in your city, in the river?"

"Yes?"

"Many of our children never learn to swim properly. That is unexpected, isn't it?"

"He probably didn't drown."

"Oh?"

"His head and hands, and feet, they weren't there in the river with him."

"I see." The officer was thrown off his game for a moment by this altered image of the boy.

"The other parts, were they found?" he asked.

"Yes."

"Where?"

"The police are keeping that close. It is a fact that few but the killer, or killers, would know. They haven't told us."

"And you think the killer was someone from here?"

"We don't think. We were here to ask questions, gather evidence. Show the boy's picture around. Try to establish where he is from. Maybe find his mother."

The interrogator stood up again, started pacing back and forth in the small room.

"Your other . . . interest. Those activities have ceased under our government," he stated.

"Which?"

"That is in the past. Those methods. Group sweeps. They are no longer necessary."

"I could interpret that—"

"Yes, interpret."

He paced more quickly.

"Children," he said. "How they must be protected. How they must be disciplined. Do you have children of your own? Back in your city?"

"No. Not yet anyway."

"Your wife said that she was not able."

"That's not exactly it."

He sat down again.

"Have you ever had cause to doubt the loyalty of your wife?" he asked. "Her loyalty to you?"

I didn't answer.

"Have you ever had cause to experience the limits of your loyalty to her?"

I didn't answer.

"Did you have sex with one of our women?"

"No."

"None?"

"None."

"Did you ever think you could be a killer? Like who killed your boy?"

"No."

He stared at me for a while again, then said, "The head and hands. The feet. You left that out."

He handed me a pen and my statement, to which I added: "The body was found floating in the river. The head and hands, and feet were found elsewhere."

He turned my statement around, checked my clarification.

"There," he said. "That boy won't be running." Then the officer pocketed the pen, stood up, folded my statement, and left the room with it.

I sat. My wife was on the other side of the wall I was looking at, in her separate room. I believed she was facing me, looking at me through the wall between us.

Some time later the door opened. Three young men came just inside, in standard national police jumpsuits, but theirs had been dyed black, and they had black boots and black berets, and on each of their shoulders was the police ID patch, should have been bright green and gold, but their patches had been dyed, too, to shades of black and dark gray, as if soaked in oil or night. And their faces had been swiped with blades of black, brown, and deep green camouflage grease. Why all that, here in this building? Behind them, my most recent interrogator was looking at me with administrative eyes.

This group moved me out the door, down a corridor, past a door open to the room my wife was in. I could see that she was seated, not facing the same wall I'd been facing, the wall between our rooms, but turned ninety degrees, looking out a window, her back to the door.

The interrogator and the three paramilitaries pushed and shoved me on down the corridor to a third room. On the way in, I noted a crudely made sign over the door: THE ROOM OF MIRACLE VISIONS. They sat me in a chair, then came back with my wife, sat her in the chair beside me, and left us alone. She didn't smile at me. There was one remaining chair in the room, no table.

"Looks a bit free-form in here," I said.

"I saw a blimp," she said.

"A blimp?"

"Out the window of that other room. Did you?"

"No, no blimp."

"And I saw a body fall out of it."

"Are you sure?"

"Yes. I saw a blimp over the harbor, and a body fell out of it, with a bundle, something heavy, pulling the body down by the feet. And I heard a yell, a shout, just faint, out there. The bundle and the body fell into the water. Did you hear anything?"

"Not like that. Any sign on the blimp? A name? Advertising?"

"Something faded and painted over, but poorly. Looked like it had been the tire company."

"Maybe a miracle vision," I said.

"Hmm?"

"The name of this room, the sign over the door."

"I didn't see a sign."

"I'll show you on the way out. When we get out. Whenever that is . . ."

Then I noticed a microphone in the upper corner of the room, next to the TV monitor. I pointed to the mike. My wife nodded. We shut up.

The TV screen was filled for a moment with the face of their president, showing concern.

Some time after that, my most recent interrogator came into the room, took the loose chair, moved it around to sit opposite us.

"Time has passed," he said.

"We noticed," I said.

"That is a way of saying time has died here. But time is something we have plenty of."

He stared at my wife, then at me.

"The other officers say I lack a sense of humor. Hmm? What do you think?"

We didn't answer. He pointed to his watch.

"We are near the hour for today's flight out. To your city."

Then he extended his hand toward us, the receiving side turned up. There were ink stains on his palm and fingers, in multiple layers, some faded from washing and time.

"Your money bleeds," I said.

He smiled, waggled his fingers like a sea eel luring a fish.

"We're broke," I said. "You've searched us. Other people got to us first."

"Well, we know what we know," he said. He looked at my wife as if they had made a deal.

"Another slow day," he lamented, then stood up and went out.

He'd left the door open. With some hesitation, we went through it, out into the corridor, which was empty. "'The Room of Miracle Visions,'" I said, "the sign." I pointed above the door. My wife looked. No sign.

24   *Not Long Ago Persons Found*

Down the corridor, we saw our luggage, thrown into a pile near the door to the street. We went to it. It had all been thoroughly rifled through, except that in the trunk of biological samples, they had not discovered the false bottom, had not opened the hidden compartments. We dragged our bags out the door and down the street to the jitney to the airport.

THE TERRACES

Before that, before the interrogations, on a day not on our itinerary, not the itinerary the governments had, we'd met with some other people, a few of them local, and in a place on a high terrace that they'd led us to, we'd dug, in the rain again that day, which could not be avoided, as it was the first of only two days we had for that site. Soon enough we were in a pit, a trench, my wife directing picks and shovels and brooms, and emerging from the earth were human bones, skulls, arms, legs, some teeth, exposed like the roots of plants, endless roots, too deep to fathom, too deep to get them all. We photographed and noted and cataloged what we could of the remains, as they were positioned, our records and a few samples labeled in code and slipped into our metal trunk, into the flat pockets under the trunk's false bottom.

This was our other work, off record, and it took us to a few such sites, on small high terraces with views down to the river, staggering our way parallel to the current, the terraces with these graves like the footprints of a malignant giant stepping down the river valley toward the last terrace, the largest, the location of the capital and the airport, overlooking the termination of the river at the ocean.

We kept quiet about these non-days, our not-work. We didn't discuss it, striving for a functional numbness. But one night, after one group grave indistinguishable from the others, my wife, the scientist, was inconsolable, pushing away my hands, demanding to be left alone, sitting at the table in the next room, sobbing, talking to herself. My wife, alone, in a cold wind she might not come out of.

The following morning, she treated me like a stranger.

"It's not you," she did say. "Not something you've done."

"Okay, but . . ."

"You must have wondered why I do this work," she went on. "That there must be something in my past. Surely you've thought that."

"Yes."

"But I'm telling you no, not in my lifetime, not my parents or their parents, nothing in my personal history, nothing in yours, either, that I know of."

"No."

"We've had it easy. There's only what we've heard, what we've read, the news."

"Right."

"But when I talk to you, even you, whom I love the most, I feel it: no safety. Don't you feel it? No safety."

"But . . ."

"You know what else? We are a violent species. People did this. We're people. Truth is, under different circumstances, you or I might have ended up on either side of something like this. So what hope is there? We excavate a trench of murdered people. Our civilization is sitting on trenches and trenches of murdered people. What's going to put a stop to this? We analyze, we document, we accuse, we want justice . . . We have our little construct back in the city. But I could destroy you. And what would make it all stop? The facts? The truth?"

Then she stopped, went cold, stood up.

"But this, what we're up to here, I don't know what else I could do, what else we could do."

She looked right at me, finally.

"If we don't get some kind of proof, the people who did these things can go on lying about it," she said. "So no, no, we'll get them. We're going to hang them with science."

She slipped a few final notes into the samples case, closed the false bottom.

"Okay?" she said.

"Okay."

And then we prepared, that day, to return to our sanctioned work: to go out into the village where we were, to show around a picture of the boy whose body had been found in our city, to ask questions. We thought we might be in or near the exact place he was from, Township C on our schematic map.

TWO POLICEMEN

"Do you know this boy? Have you seen him? Do you know his mother, his father? Do you know anybody in his family?"

And so forth, showing the boy's picture around and around the small town, the marketplace. Some cautious looks, but no results, no new clues. Then on a side street our way was blocked by two men in the uniforms of the local police, one with more decorations on it than the other.

"Do you know this boy?" we asked, et cetera, et cetera, handing the photograph to the more decorated one, the senior officer. He didn't look at the picture, handed it back to me.

"So . . . found in your river," he said.

"Yes."

"You may be surprised what we know," he said.

We didn't react.

"Many of these boys and girls never learn to swim properly," he went on. "It is paradoxical, they live so close to water—"

"He probably didn't drown," my wife interrupted. "Evidence is, he was killed elsewhere, then the body dumped in the river."

"I see. And your suspect is here?"

"We don't know," I said.

I handed the photo to the junior officer. The senior officer was becoming agitated, distracting me. I didn't observe the junior officer's reaction to the picture. I hoped my wife would.

"We start by trying to determine where the boy is from," I said. "From here? This region? This town? This street?"

"That exact?" The junior officer spoke for the first time.

The senior officer broke in. "These boys are dead anyway, the ones who leave. Even if they come back, they are dead."

"Hmm," I said.

"Hmm," my wife said.

The senior officer turned and walked away. The junior officer lingered a moment, looking at the picture, then up at us, expressionless. Then he handed the photo back to me and followed his superior down the street.

We continued with our inquiries. Half an hour later, we sensed that we were being followed. We cut down an alley to the next street over, reversed our direction, ducked into a shop, waited, returned to the street, turned a corner, and came up face-to-face with the junior officer, expressionless as before.

"We would like to invite you to our offices," he said.

"Invite?" I asked.

"It has begun to rain. Why don't you come inside for a break?"

Ten minutes later, the junior officer let us into his private office, a tiny room with salvaged desk and chairs, and, in the upper corner, a new large-screen television, hanging from the ceiling on a bracket, the volume on low, like a small brook in a meadow, the images, as we came in, of a large face talking, soldiers emerging from a helicopter, suspects being thrown to the ground, suspects wearing mixed athletic gear, from different sports and countries, like a starved post-Olympics team that had competed, after the final whistle, to grab clothing from what the athletes left behind.

The junior officer looked up at the TV. His expression soured.

"We are expected to leave it on," he said.

We'd been thoroughly drenched by the rain. I bent down to pull the fabric of my pants away from my calf. The thin, wet material was stuck against my skin like a plastic bag sucked in around a person's face. When I straightened up, the junior officer said, "Our money bleeds."

I tilted my head inquiringly. He pointed to my hat. When I took it off, we could see that the rain had soaked through the top of the hat and into the currency I'd folded and hidden in the interior pocket up there, and ink from the bills had begun to seep back up into the flat fabric of the hat crown, a few faint lines and splotches emerging like ghosts.

"When it rains, our money bleeds," he elaborated. "Sorry, local joke. It doesn't translate well."

I stood holding the hat, slightly discolored drips from it falling to the floor, disappearing into the porous and already stained concrete.

"We don't have much time," the junior officer said. "Remove the bills, put one back in the hat, give the rest to me."

I hesitated.

"You have no choice but to trust me," he said. "Now. We have no time."

I took the money out of the hat pocket, put one small-denomination bill back, held the hat, handed him the rest of our stash.

"And your pants pockets?" he asked.

I told him I had one small bill there. In fact, I had three. These were left in place. He looked at my wife. She handed him the bills from her shirt pocket. He flipped off one for her to put back, folded her other bills together with the bills from my hat, bent over to place the remaining bulk of our cash into a drawer of his desk. He jerked his head to get me to drop the hat on the side table; then he straightened up and put on a big smile. Not for us. Exactly then, the door burst open and the senior officer strode into the room.

"Junior Officer, have you searched our guests?" he asked.

"Just getting started, sir," the junior officer replied. Then he asked me to empty my pockets onto his desk and patted me down and turned to face my wife.

"Just empty your pockets," he said to her.

The senior officer was beginning to look with interest at my wife, at her thin, soaked clothing. The junior officer caught the senior officer's eye and led the man's gaze away from my wife and toward my hat on the table. As the senior officer considered the hat, the junior officer fingered through the things from our pockets. He picked up the bill that had come from my wife's pocket and the three bills from my pocket. He held up my three bills, splayed, glancing at me to note my fib that I had only one. All in an instant.

"The hat!" the senior officer boomed.

"Of course, sir. Yes, I see."

The junior officer removed the bill from the hat crown, added that to the bills from our pockets, held them all up. The senior officer took them. That left the majority of our cash untouched in the junior officer's desk.

"We will keep these as a deposit," the senior officer said, fingering through the bills in his hand. "Against the charges to you for police services."

He turned to leave, turned back.

"Junior Officer," he said with a half smile, tipping his head.

Then he walked behind the desk, stood beside the junior officer.

"Top drawer!" the senior officer commanded.

The junior officer calmly opened the top drawer of his desk. The senior officer looked in.

"Bottom drawer!" the senior officer commanded.

Same routine.

"Keeping you honest, Junior Officer, ha-ha!" the senior officer laughed. Then he folded our wet money into a handkerchief, slid the handkerchief into his shirt pocket, and strode out of the room.

The junior officer closed the door, grinned at us for the first time. The TV murmured. Now soldiers were jumping down from a transport truck, rifles ready, fanning out toward an enemy not seen. We sat down at the junior officer's desk. There was an uncertain calm, as in the moment after a car crash.

"He never asks for the middle drawer," the junior officer said.

"So now," he continued, "let's review. You are showing the victim's picture around, does anybody know him, does anybody know his family."

"Yes," I replied.

"Any results?"

"Nothing . . . definite," I said.

Nothing much, actually.

"We are also collecting biological samples," my wife said. "Physical evidence, for analysis in our city, in connection with the boy's death, the boy in the picture."

"Yes. What evidence?"

"Samples of air and water, samples of seeds and flowers, samples of bones from local animals, samples of earth and stones, small bits of dirt and dust."

"Air, water, seeds, flowers, bones, earth, stones, soil," the junior officer repeated. "Pollen analysis? Bone-mineral analysis?"

My wife smiled for the first time in days. She leaned forward.

"That's it," she said.

"What is the geographic range of your inquiry?"

"Our palynologist . . ." she started, then paused, looking at the junior officer, her one eyebrow lifted and the opposite eyelid half closed, as she does. The junior officer paused, too, savoring the moment.

"Your palynologist . . . your pollen specialist," he said.

"Yes."

My wife smiled again. She grabbed the pen and notepad lying to one side of the junior officer's desk, then began to explain the details, making marks on the paper as she talked—lines, arcs, bullet points, arrows, short slashes, filled circles, no words, just shapes and a few numbers on the pad. This was what she did when talking about science, when she was happy. Soon enough, the junior officer opened his top desk drawer, took out his one other pen, began adding his own marks to the paper between them.

"But the palynologist was after the geophysicist," my wife was saying. "When we knew nothing, we started with the bone minerals."

"The strontium 90 profile," the junior officer said.

"Yes."

"The strontium 90 profile of the boy's bones tracked to the profile of our minerals here, the geology of a region like ours."

"Yes."

"And your samples of local minerals and bones will give you a confirmation."

"Yes. But on minerals only, it could be more than one area of the globe—with that geology. Still not exact."

"So you intersect the geology with the palynology."

"Right. In our city, before we traveled. Based on grass and tree pollen found in the boy's lungs, in his nasal passages, on his skin, where those several different pollens all occur in one place, we narrowed it down to some part of this river valley."

"Then with the samples you collect here, you narrow it further."

"Exactly," my wife said, so happy while so close to such a grim subject.

The junior officer looked wistfully out his small window for a moment.

"So you have an electron microscope, a spectrometer, a radiometer," he said.

"Oh yes."

"I am envious," the junior officer said. "We lack equipment here. I have access to one optical microscope, in the next town. I can barely estimate the age of blood at a crime scene. I can only guess at the origins of stomach contents. We spent what budget there was on these televisions. They were required."

The junior officer looked up at the TV. His expression soured again. We turned in our seats. On the screen were soldiers prodding women with their hands up into a transport truck, the voice-over sounding aroused, even at low volume.

36   *Not Long Ago Persons Found*

"But tell me, please, which of our trees were the indicators? How do you account for wind currents? Could you tell the season he'd left, how long he'd been away . . ."

And they were off again, talking and gesturing and marking the sheet of paper. The pollen that the boy had breathed in included species of grasses widespread in their river valley, but grass pollen can travel some distance in the wind, so that left the geographic extent still too broad. So then they also referenced the boy's pollen to pollen from three types of trees. Tree pollen is heavier, isn't spread so far by breezes as it drops. And there were only a few locations in the valley where those trees lived together with one another and with those grasses.

Later, the pollen mix in his stomach and intestines could be used to estimate how recently he'd eaten food from his home—ate it here before he left, or brought it with him, or was given it after he arrived—compared to how many days he'd been eating food from around our city. And the pollen types on his clothes, did they include some from our city? Was he wearing his original clothing, what he traveled in, or, in the time in our city, had he changed clothes, or had his clothes been changed for him before the body ended up in the river?

At the end of half an hour, the sheet of paper in front of them was covered with the marks they had made while talking. The junior officer was about to lift off that sheet and start on a new page. He paused.

"So all this. You have a general idea of a locale in our country that he is from, you estimate how long he'd been in your city, and you have some hints as to his contacts after he arrived there?"

"Yes."

"Then what?"

"Well, something else. In his stomach, a partially digested mash including beans of a type that can be used to induce partial paralysis. The subject can think and breathe but cannot move."

This was one of the details that was supposed to be kept close.

"I see," the junior officer said.

He thought for a moment, then used his remote to turn up the volume on the TV, and signaled to us to lean in close.

"The body," he said, "was it intact when it was found?"

This, too, was a detail we were supposed to keep quiet.

"The head and hands . . ." the junior officer went on.

"Found elsewhere," my wife confided.

"Mm-hmm," the junior officer said. "And now what?"

"We continue to show his picture around; we hope to find his family. In any case, when we return to our city, we analyze and compare the biological and mineral samples; we get or confirm a more exact fix on the place that he's from. Then they will send us or somebody like us to that place, maybe back here, to ask more questions."

"Yes, of course."

"To make further inquiries."

"Yes."

"Yes. And . . ." my wife began.

"Something else?" the junior officer asked.

"There are other applications. For this. The science," she said.

"Yes?"

My wife looked at the junior officer for a long, uncomfortable time and he looked at her, his eyes like pools of water, giving nothing back.

"We are interested in the disappearances," she said.

The junior officer said nothing; his expression didn't change. Then he leaned in closer.

"The police in your city have taken an interest in our country? They have time?" he asked.

"Not the police. Another organization."

"So many 'other organizations.'"

"This one is on your side."

"How do you know what my side is? You should be very careful."

She started to speak again, but the junior officer wiped his hand through the air to put a stop to it. He tore off the sheet with all their marks on it, laid it aside. He wrote out an address on the clean sheet of paper underneath, tore that off, handed it to my wife. He held up the notepad, tilted it, studying the indents from what he'd just written. He tore off the next two blank sheets, crumpled them, tossed them into the corner of the room, under the TV. His face was troubled. He looked up at my wife, who was holding the paper he'd written the address on.

"You should go to that shop," he said quietly. "Show your picture, ask your questions."

"Can we say you sent us?"

"You'd better not. Please put that address away."

Then the junior officer stood up, moderated the TV volume with his remote.

"Thank you for coming," he said, loud and clear, over the TV.

He noticed me looking at the page of scribbles that he and my wife had made as they were talking. It was still on his desk, to the side. Why had he not disposed of that?

"They could ask to see my notes," he explained in a whisper. "Don't worry, they'll never understand any of it." As it turned out, he was right about that, too.

Next the junior officer opened the middle drawer of his desk, took out our cash bundle. Following his gestures, we separated the bills into four flat sets, one set for each of our ankles, my wife's and mine, wrapped just above the anklebone, under the sock, under the pant leg.

Finally, back to a loud, clear voice, he said, "Now we will return to the front desk to record your visit and dismiss you."

The junior officer herded us out of his room, down a corridor, to the intake hall. As he was making notes in the log there, we saw the senior officer to one side, facing a man who was smaller than him but more confident, and not wearing a uniform. The senior officer was talking fast and smiling; then he stopped. The shorter man reached up, took a handkerchief from the senior officer's pocket, the handkerchief that held the cash that had been confiscated from us. The shorter man gave one bill back to the senior officer, then put the handkerchief with the other bills into his own shirt pocket, then turned to us, smiled, and disappeared down a corridor.

"Yes, my friends," the senior officer said cheerfully, coming toward us. He escorted us out the door and onto the street. We stood all together for a moment in the afternoon shadow cast by the police station, the senior officer between the two of us, his arms stretched out so that one hand was on my shoulder, one hand on my wife's shoulder. He turned to me and spoke with his big voice. "Your wife is a biological anthropologist, you are her assistant," he recited to me. "You are here to gather evidence. Have you seen the boy in this picture, do you know him, do you know anybody in his family . . . Hmm? Ha-ha!"

We smiled. He lowered his head, pulled us in closer, dropped his voice down to what was, for him, a confidential, conspiratorial rumble. "What else? Hmm? Ha-ha!"

"We're still looking," I said.

"Yes. What else?"

"We're about done here," my wife offered.

The senior officer looked at her, then back to me.

"The disappearances, the time of the disappearances," he said. "There are those who say the disappeared have all gone up above the river, that they are on the terraces, up there, like that one."

With his chin he pointed to one of the terraces visible above the roofs of the buildings across the street. We looked up there. He squeezed our shoulders. We looked back at him.

"Some say that is where they disappeared to. I suppose if that were so, you could go and look."

We had. We would.

"Go and look for them, ha-ha! If that is where they are. And what will you find? Ghosts and imaginings. Old things. Go and look."

His voice had suddenly ramped back up to its full public volume. He looked around at the few people passing by on the street.

"The past!" he declared, smiling. "That is all in the past. It is over. That does not happen in the present time. This government, our government, put a stop to that long ago. We are progressive! We have your support!"

He stopped, pulled my wife and me in even closer, and spoke quietly again. "Those practices have not been used for years. They are no longer necessary."

He gave me, then my wife, a meaningful look.

"But go," he said. "Go to your ghosts, go dig."

Then he released his grip on our shoulders, dropped his arms, scanned the street to see who was looking, turned, and went back inside the police station.

My wife and I walked two blocks down, one block over, checked if we were being followed, stopped at a wall on the shadowed side of the street.

"So the terraces, no bodies there, and oh, those bodies, that's the past," I said.

"Right."

Then my wife pulled from her pocket the paper given to her by the junior officer, and we looked at the address he'd written on it.

EVERY MAN AND WOMAN A THEORIST

At the shop at that address, they were selling whatever they could get cheap. Vacation clothes on racks outside, luggage hanging on the wide-open doors. And inside, more luggage, dominating the front half of the high-ceilinged space, columns of airport rollers in more colors and sizes than we thought possible in that small town. The proprietor had a long pole with a hook, which he used to catch a piece of luggage by its handle and move it from one perch to another in his displays. We watched as he poled one suitcase, then another through the air, as though he were preparing them for the sensation of flying.

We showed him the picture, asked the questions.

"Yes," he said.

"Yes what?" I asked.

"He took one of those," he said.

He pointed with his pole up to the smallest of the rolling suitcases, in blue; then he flew it down and landed it on the counter between us. He put the boy's picture on top of the empty suitcase and looked up at us.

"I sold one of these to his mother. Then she disappeared."

"You're sure?" my wife asked.

"Why wouldn't I be?" he replied.

"Do you know his family?"

"They've disappeared."

"Disappeared," my wife repeated.

"At about the same time that the boy left."

"What do you mean disappeared, then? Did you know them?"

The proprietor's wife spoke up, looking at her husband. "He did not know them; we did not. Some say that the family went north, left the country. Some say that they disappeared. Disappeared," the woman repeated, looking carefully at us. "We don't know. We have heard, from some, that the boy may have become separated, may have traveled separately from his family. With one of these excellent suitcases."

"He had an uncle living abroad," the proprietor said. "We heard."

"Living where?" my wife asked.

The man shrugged his shoulders. There was a world map under the glass on the counter. I pointed to our city on it.

"Here?" I asked.

"Maybe there."

"Why did he leave?" I asked. "How? Seven years old."

"We just sell luggage," the wife said. "To carry many things, to go many places, as the owner desires."

"What has this boy done?" the proprietor asked.

"He's dead," my wife said.

"Oh," the proprietor and his wife said together. Then they went silent for a moment, unreadable.

"How did he die?" the proprietor asked.

"He was found in our river," I said.

"Drowned? They can't swim, these children."

"The police believe he was killed. Elsewhere. Then dumped in the river."

"Was the body. . . intact?" the proprietor asked.

"Not exactly," my wife said.

They went silent again. Then the proprietor's wife looked at her husband and pointed with her chin out the door and down the street to the right. The proprietor nodded, took a scrap of paper from under the counter, wrote on it at some length, handed it to us, together with the photo of the boy.

"Go to this shop," he said.

"Can we say you sent us?" I asked.

"You'd better not," the proprietress said. "Could you leave this way, please?"

She came from behind the counter and led us toward the back of the shop. The proprietor picked up the empty suitcase from the counter and flew it back up to its perch among the others. The proprietor's wife let us out the back door to the alley behind the store.

Afternoon was beginning to fall into evening. We picked a direction, walked the alley's length out to a street, stood in one of the last remnants of sun, and studied the address the travel shop owner had written out for us:

Gift Shop
Church of Saint Thomas
Cinnamon Street
across from the bookstore named
Sun and Moon

We walked a block or two this way and that, got to where we couldn't find any street signs. We didn't know where we were or how to find the shop on Cinnamon Street. We stopped a child, a little girl, playing in front of a house. I showed her the address, read it aloud to her, asked her for directions. She said we should follow her, and she took off without further discussion.

As we turned along streets and alleys and steps up a hill, the girl got farther and farther from us. We thought she looked back occasionally, as if increasing the distance was her intention. Then she disappeared altogether. We stopped.

"Oh," my wife said, startled by something, but then relieved.

I followed her gaze. We later agreed that what we'd seen, what we thought we saw, was the boy from our photo, in shorts, no shirt, no shoes, walking ahead of us on the street, his head, hands, and feet rejoined to his body at thin red lines, as if glued, the different parts moving not entirely in sync. But he was walking, back in his home. We followed, along streets, around corners. Then he, too, disappeared. We stopped.

It was getting dark. Halfway up the block we were on, we saw a sign for the bookstore, Sun and Moon, and across from it, the gift shop for the Church of St. Thomas. We went to the gift shop door. Even at this late hour, there was light inside, dim, some of it from candles. We tried the door. It was unlocked. We went in. There was a man at a counter, halfway into the shop, looking at us as we came in.

"Yes, yes, yes," he said. "Um-hmm."

We showed him the picture, asked the first questions.

"Did the police send you?" he asked back.

"Not—" my wife started.

"No. Not exactly," I finished.

The clerk looked back and forth between my wife and me. I showed him his address, given to us by the travel shop owner.

"This is who sent us. Do you recognize the handwriting?" I asked.

"Why would I say yes?" he responded.

So I tried this: "Small blue suitcase," I said.

The clerk turned toward one of the shop windows, as if somebody might be there, outside. We saw no one. After some time, the clerk turned back, examined the two of us thoroughly up and down, then looked me in the eye for some time, then looked my wife in the eye for some time. Apparently, we passed. Somewhat.

"The police know nothing," he stated. "When they look at the river, they see only water. They don't see the old events, rising up, the unsatisfied. They know only what they can put in jail. That is why people are afraid of them."

"Yes," I said.

The clerk looked at me like he didn't believe I knew what I was saying yes to.

Then my wife pointed again to the picture of the boy in front of the clerk, and began again to tell the story, ask all the questions. I ventured away to other parts of the shop. Standard church retail, local edition, I guessed, except in one section where there were shelves with plant roots and barks in large glass jars; seeds, beans, and herbs in smaller jars; objects and figurines in wood, cloth, and clay; two small drums; and a few books that I doubted were consistent with current church doctrine. When I returned to the counter, the clerk was staring at the picture of the boy.

"So. Do you know him?" my wife asked again.

"Perhaps."

"Perhaps?"

"Perhaps."

"Perhaps? Please . . ."

"This one, or ones like him, like this, like that . . . How did he die? What do your police say?"

I touched my wife's arm to keep her quiet about this.

"It's all preliminary," I said.

"So they don't know." The clerk looked back and forth between us again, then said, "Death could have been placed in him here, to come out later, there."

"A curse?" my wife asked.

48   *Not Long Ago Persons Found*

"A curse, yes. Or something he saw. So then later, because he believed he would die, he died. Was the body intact?"

"Hmm?"

"Was the body in one piece? All the parts of it."

"We don't have the details," my wife said, dodging.

"It could be that somebody from here, living there, would cut off and separate the head, hands, and feet, if the death was unnatural, to prevent the spirit from roaming, to prevent the spirit from causing harm to others, to prevent the spirit from being used."

"They haven't told us," she claimed again. "A curse, is that something you would know how to do?"

"Alternately," the clerk said, ignoring her question, "not a curse. The boy could have been sacrificed, directly. Somebody from here living there, or somebody who pursued the boy to your city, or had him delivered, could have sacrificed the boy."

"Why?"

"For success, for money, to get power over their landlord. Stupid things, often as not."

The clerk signaled to us to follow him to the special section of the shop. Between two shelves there, he lowered his voice and said, "I saw a flock of birds turning around the face of the mother. She was coming upstream, in the middle of the river, looking for her son, her boy. To protect him. But she couldn't because he was in your city."

"You saw this when?" I asked.

"Some time ago," the clerk said.

"When you say you saw the mother . . ." my wife

began. "What do you mean? Was it something we could see?" She pointed to the two of us.

"If you look. If you know how," the clerk replied.

"How? How would we look?"

The clerk contemplated her with some interest but didn't reply.

Then the clerk turned, pointed to a bottle on a shelf, containing small brown beans.

"If the boy was sacrificed, they could have started with beans like these," he said. "The beans paralyze the animal first. That is important, if it is done as it is supposed to be done."

"This was a boy, not an animal," my wife said.

"Yes. There are dark practitioners, too," the clerk said.

"Have you sold any of these beans recently?" I asked.

"Anybody can buy them," the clerk replied.

"But . . . Okay, okay," my wife said. "Do you know any local . . . practitioners, traditional healers, who might have been involved in what happened to this boy? Were you involved?"

"We have heard something. Of his fate. But it was not us," the clerk said.

Then he took down a glass jar with coils of red strings in it. He pulled one string out, held it by the end. It was blood red, with three yellow bands woven in near the end that he held.

"You could look for one of these," he said. "He would have worn it for protection."

"If so, it didn't work," I said.

The clerk offered the string to my wife, then me. We declined. The clerk returned the string to its jar, and from a different shelf, he brought down a small clay bottle, which he handed to my wife. The bottle was corked tight, but it seemed to be empty. It was a natural clay color, slightly flattened on two sides, and on each flat plane a glazed bird's head, in profile, the head black on one side, white on the other.

"You could look for something like that," he said. "He could have taken something like it to your city. To have it with him, or to deliver it to someone else, a gift."

It was late. The shop was getting dark. We hadn't eaten since morning. The clay bottle seemed to glow and murmur in my wife's hand.

"Oh no," she said, and put the bottle back on the shelf.

The clerk gestured for us to come closer and lowered his voice further, to a whisper.

"The boy's parents are dead. He went to your city to find his uncle. That is what I've heard. And now, I've said too much. If you tell anyone from whom it was that you heard these things, my fate will be sealed, and it will not be pretty. It's late. I must close. Come."

He led us back to the counter, took out a notepad, wrote something on it, gave the paper to my wife.

"On your way to the airport, when you leave, when you get to the capital, go to this shop. They might have something more for you."

"Can we say you sent us?" she asked.

"That won't be necessary."

He herded us toward the door.

"Or the boy could simply have been killed, for some other no-good reason. Murdered," he said. "Don't put him back together."

"Hmm?" I asked.

"Don't put the parts of him all together in one place."

We didn't tell him they'd already done that. He pushed us out and shut and locked the shop door as we stood out on the street, looking in.

"He knows more," I said.

"Or thinks he does."

NOT LONG AGO PERSONS FOUND

The day after our visit to the church shop was the beginning of one of the blocks of non-days on our itinerary. Our local contacts led us to a terrace not far downriver from Township C. We started to dig, all of us, and it soon became obvious that, as they'd told us, the bodies there had been buried recently, within the last year. In the terms of the trade, the remains were partially skeletonized. The flesh was not entirely gone, many teeth, both front and back, still remained in jaws. And so forth.

As the earth cover was removed, the stench of rotting corpses rose and filled the meadow. Some from our group left the dig a few times to vomit, to weep, vomit, weep, repeat, until nothing was left. So much for incidents like this being in the long ago. The clothing, the paraphernalia, the postures of many of the bodies could still be read. Some of these people had been alive at the moment the dirt was pushed in over them.

From that site we could see, down through gaps in the trees, a small market town, and flashes of moving water, the river. So anybody down there could look up between the shaded stalls, between the buildings, and see this terrace where the unidentified had been interred, with people now digging them up.

One of our group, clearing away from the trench to breathe some fresh air, found indications of three people from one side or the other of this incident who had lived through it and left the scene, on foot, at least one of them with some kind of wound or wounds. These three had set out on a path that led farther down the river. On the afternoon of the final of our non-days at this site, we decided that while my wife got the last of what she could get, in that time frame, from that grave, I and two trackers would try to follow the trail of those who had walked away.

The traces that they'd left were splots of dried blood on plant leaves and the ground, and intermittent clusters of distinctive footprints where mud had dried undisturbed since the rainy season—prints from two pairs of similar boots and one pair of simple sandals. Their route paralleled the river for a few kilometers. Then, at a point where the river canyoned through a dry ridge, the walking path was forced to the side, up an empty gully, a ravine, diverging from the cut of the main watercourse.

We pursued the tracks up the gully, the blood splots more frequent, the gully ever up, steeper and narrower, the late afternoon sinking behind us. Through the gap where the gully reached the ridgetop, we perceived a sky glow of a dirtier color than the last sunlight at our backs, and when we got to the top, what lay before us was the sprawl and scattered roar of the capital city, on the coast, lights coming on, cheap orange anti-crime lights, sparse and sulfurous on streets and lots, and smaller kitchen lights, alley lights, truck lights, with humanity packed between. The traces of our three subjects wandered down the slope before us toward the outskirts of the city. Whomever it was that we were after, those individuals could have disappeared into the urbanizing below just as easily as disappearing into a jungle. That's what many of them were doing down there: disappearing.

We returned to the excavation in the dark. My wife and the other volunteers were still working, endurance and the floodlight batteries running out. Around midnight we wrapped up, refilled the trench, and left. Even after several days there, we couldn't be sure we had uncovered or counted them all, but, estimating, we called that site the grave of forty plus three. The plus three were probably supposed to have been buried there, too, but appeared to have escaped.

THE WALTZ OF THE WALLS

Our time to leave. We went to the capital city; we stood in line at our consulate; we stood in line at a bank; we stood in line at the post office, to mail picture postcards, as people would, but our messages were coded.

Two persons ahead of us in line at the post office was a round woman with a round child, the child in a wire cage on two wheels, the woman's rolling shopping basket. The child standing, singing, holding the wire wall to balance, then plopping down to the blanket at the bottom, to sit and stare at another child, older, also in the line.

The younger child shared the cage with—rested one shoulder against—a large cube wrapped in brown paper, an address handwritten on it in large letters, twice, on opposite sides. The round woman lifted out the cube, put it on the counter in front of the postal clerk. The round child was amazed and gaping for a moment at the void left by the removed package.

On the counter, one of the addresses on the package now faced us. It read:

Gift Shop
Church of Saint Thomas

56   *Not Long Ago Persons Found*

Cinnamon Street

across from

Sun and Moon Books

. . . in the town upriver that we'd just left. If we wanted to find that shop again, we could mail ourselves to it.

The postal clerk looked at the address, took payment from the woman, processed the package, placed it on the counter behind him, against a partial wall. He took an additional payment from the woman, dropped that into a cloth sack hanging on the side of his booth. He called out. The young man who came from behind the wall to pick up the package was wearing not the blue uniform of the postal service but the black soaked and dyed jumpsuit of the special forces of the national police, his pants tucked into his boots, ready to wade through a scatter of biting corpses.

The round woman went wide-eyed when she saw who it was that picked up her package. She hurried out, her wire basket with the child getting caught in the door, then yanked free.

We mailed our postcards. And for after that, we had blocked out three hours of unreported time to go to the shop we'd been referred to by the clerk in the church shop upriver, the clerk who might soon receive a package delivered by the police. We thought that from that shop, in the capital, we might be able to get a warning back up the river to the clerk.

At the address he'd given us, we went in a door, which jangled a bell. The shop had been emptied. Sitting at the cleared-off counter were two young policemen, teenagers, surprised to see us but quickly snapping to, putting on a menacing mien, and following procedure to deliver us to headquarters. That was how we'd got to where we'd been interrogated—the first time—and we'd made our formal statements about the boy in the photograph, and then we'd slipped out, by their plan or their negligence, and boarded the jitney, with all our luggage and the samples case intact, on our way to the airport. All, just the first time.

Before checking in at the ticket counter of the national airline, we found our way to a dead room in a part of the airport that had been abandoned mid-expansion. We backed a trash crate against the door, lay on the construction-littered floor, and made love, had sex. My wife sometimes tried to counter nihilism in this way. She was fond of risky behavior, was aroused by it. Me, too. As it turned out, that time, that place, was one of our best. We had each other, our momentary beauty, our fragile bodies that could so easily be turned against us, that could be made to feel eradicating pain and fear.

Then, standing in line to board that day's flight to our city, we were pulled out and driven back to police headquarters. As we were escorted in, the TV monitors in the entry hall were showing a military parade. It included seven men, hooded, hands tied behind them, sitting on a bench on a flatbed truck.

We were separated and interrogated again, again the questions about our other project, again they just stopped, and we left for the airport—the second attempt. Then the whole procedure was repeated: pulled from the airport, back to the police, to the airport, to the police . . . all of us on both sides playing dumber and dumber, the possibility of physical harm to us made clearer. We had thought that our passports, our consulate would protect us from the worst. That thought was obsolete. In the new era, the concept was no protection for anybody, now that it was known worldwide that our country had no integrity in its treatment of others.

So we understood, though not much was said, when we were reunited another time in what had been the Room of Miracle Visions, in the central police station, now with a new sign over the door saying CONFERENCE 1. There were still only loose chairs in there, no table, the room adaptable to many actions.

"Sorry you missed today's flight. Again," our new interrogator said, as happy as a jackal. "We're sending you back to the airport."

"Sure. Our tickets are no good. Again," I said.

"You can talk to them; you can wait, as you have before," he said. "But now there is another problem: Your visas are about to expire."

He returned our passports to us, opened both of them to a page that showed that the dates of our visas had been hand-altered, such that their authorization of our stay would end that day at midnight.

MR. FIX

We slept that night at the airport, in the same dead room we'd made love in. The next morning, we ran down our batteries trying to search for and talk to a person or persons who could realign us on the right lists so we could get out of there. No luck, and no electrical power in that room. We left for some other area of the terminal, where at least we could recharge our phones.

Turning into a main corridor, we saw, standing to one side of it, a radiating, compact, youthful man—on closer look not young, but not yet old—tanned skin, baseball hat on top of curly blond hair, dark glasses curved for the wind (if any), orange safety vest over a dark blue jumpsuit, legs spread, arms folded on his chest. He appeared to be supervising a work project that we could not see. On his safety vest, the name of a construction company of global reach.

"These are not happy campers," we heard him say.

As we went closer, on our way to pass by, he broke out a million-dollar smile, generally orienting his head in our direction. The curved sunglasses might have been his actual eyes, the eyes of a large fly or locust. If we were

59

what he was looking at, he could be seeing a thousand of us.

"Not happy at all," he ventured again.

"Do we know you?" I asked.

"You should," he replied.

"Oh?" I said.

He amped up the smile again. Perfect teeth. He could eat anything of any size. He offered a handshake to both of us.

"We need to work together, all of us. Get on the same page. Then everybody will be positivized."

"Oh?" I repeated.

"Are you with me?" he asked.

We said nothing. He ignited the smile again and held up a finger. Two locals appeared from nowhere, dark blue jumpsuits like his, minus the orange safety vest, minus the dark glasses, minus the hat, but trying hard to do the smile.

"Get their bags," he said to them. "Let's talk," he said to us. He held open a door we hadn't noticed. His assistants and our luggage went through it. We followed, as did he, closing the door behind him.

"Ticket problems?" he asked. His accent was from one of the wide regions far outside our city.

"We had valid tickets," I said. "We got in line to board; the police pulled us out for questions, downtown, where we'd already been."

"Um-hmm."

"They released us, we came back here, we pled with the airline to get on the next flight. They weren't sure when that would be. Then finally we were back in line again to board and the police pulled us out for more questions. And so forth. Then we were past our visa deadline. It's not legal for us to leave the country because it's not legal for us to be here."

"Where you staying while you wait this out?"

"We had a hotel, but we can't take the bus back there because we can't board without a room number, and we can't get a room over the phone from here."

"Fake the number," he said.

"They check."

"Right. Sleeping at the airport?"

"Not allowed."

"Well, that's not right, is it? You have not been treated right. No wonder you look so bad. This all needs to be fixed."

Then he smiled the high-dollar smile, zipped up his orange safety vest, and left the room. His two assistants stepped in front of the door, facing us, blocking us. They smiled the smile, their best approximation of it.

The room we were in was partially complete, had been partially complete for a while, the walls roughed in but not finished or painted, bits and scraps of ducts and electrical cables and other debris on the floor, a lighting fixture partway down out of the ceiling, one bulb missing from it. One window bay had blinds installed and closed. The other window bay had only a rain jacket hung and spread over it, partially blocking the view in or out. Against a raw wall was a single filing cabinet, four drawers high, and near that a conference table and four folding metal chairs, all the furniture new and finished in a matching palette of taupe and mauve, mauvish taupe.

The air in the room didn't move.

One system that seemed complete and functioning was the security surveillance, the red indicator light of a ceiling camera flicking on when we approached the jacket draped over the window, and another camera activating when we approached the file cabinet.

We waved and posed for the cameras, a little delirious. Then we lay on the floor, adding—why not—to the dust on our clothes. We fell asleep.

We woke when we heard whistling outside the door. It was dark out through the windows and dark inside the room. The sensors, detecting nothing, had let everything shut down. Our two guards were gone. We heard the beeping of the code lock on the door; then it opened and our host came in, still whistling. The radiance of his smile at us was undiminished, his bug eyes still on.

"Problem solved," he said.

We were as groggy as tired dogs.

"I do something for you, you do something for me," he continued.

"Okay," I said.

"Okay," my wife said.

"I get you on tomorrow's flight out, you give me your passports."

"What do you need to see?" I asked.

"I mean I keep them. Two valid passports, a man and

a woman, traveling together. That would be very useful. For what we're doing."

"But . . ."

"Don't worry, don't worry. You hand them over at the last minute, when you're boarding the plane. Then when you arrive in the city, you just explain: 'Lost our passports.' See? There'll be some huffing and puffing— bouf bouf bouf. Then what? Nothing. You'll be fine. I'll let them know."

"Give up our passports? How will they be used, exactly? There will be two people loose out there with our names? I don't know . . ."

"For a good cause, my friends. For our work in this country, in this part of the world."

"I don't know. From what we've seen . . ."

He dropped the smile, took off his shades. The eyes underneath were the alert blue of a ski jumper. He poked the glasses into my chest.

"Yes. What have you seen? What have you two been up to?"

We showed him the picture.

"This boy's body was found floating in the river in our city, wild pollen in his lungs from the river valley here, in this country . . ." and so forth, the rest of the story, during which he looked at the photo quickly, handed it back, and put his insect eyes back on.

"Computer composite," he said.

"Yes."

"The head was detached."

"Yes."

"Then put back on in the photo."

"Yes."

"What else?"

"We have samples in our trunk, related to the case—pollen, bones, air, soil, water. And a few leads from talking to people. Nothing definite."

"I mean what else?"

"Nothing else."

"Your other investigation. They want to know what else you've been doing. That's why they are going to keep calling you back."

"For nothing."

"I'd like to know, too, if you could help me out. There are many parties concerned for your welfare. This is not school. This is not pretend."

We were silent.

"Do you understand your situation?"

"I think so."

"No. I don't think so. For the interrogations, they separate you?"

"Yes."

"Your wife is very attractive. Your wife would be very attractive to them. Do you follow?"

"They wouldn't."

"Times have changed."

The three of us stood there, motionless long enough for the cameras to click off, the lights to dim to half. Bug Eyes lost his smile, scanned our faces, one to the other and back again. Then he moved toward the door. The lights and cameras came alive again.

"Think it over. Your passports," he said. "Food in the fridge under that counter, bathroom through that door. Think it over."

He went out. We sat on the chairs at the conference table. Flimsy chairs, scarcely able to hold us up.

"There's no camera in the bathroom," my wife observed later.

The next morning, I climbed out through the bathroom window, made a phone call standing in the partial shade of a partial roof over another incomplete part of the airport's arbitrary expansion. Some time after my return to the room, we heard whistling in the corridor outside again, then the beeping of the door-lock code.

Bug Eyes came in, ignited his solar smile, and dangled before us a single sheet of paper, the upper corner of it delicately pinched between the thumb and forefinger of a tight-stretched surgery glove, which was suffocating his right hand. On the sheet of paper were the curves, dashes, hash marks, arrows, and slashes that my wife and the junior officer had made as they talked about pollen and bone minerals and the river biome and the cut marks on the boy's body and all the rest.

"Meaning?" Bug Eyes asked.

"Just doodles. While we talked," my wife said.

"Right. Sure."

He went to the file cabinet, punched in the code, opened the top drawer, finger-walked his way to somewhere in the middle, pushed open a file folder. He waved

66   *Not Long Ago Persons Found*

us closer to look into the drawer. Our names were at the head of a thin slice of the files—three fresh manila folders for us, each almost empty. He took a last look at the marked-up sheet of paper.

"I'll send it to Code. They'll figure it out."

He dropped the page into our file, closed the drawer, snapped the glove off his hand.

"Have you come to a decision? Hmm?" he asked.

"There's a flight out this afternoon. We think we can get on it."

"Sure. Good luck."

We assumed that when we were ready, we could just push out through that door unimpeded. We sat again on the collapsible chairs to wait for a while. Mr. Fix opened the lowest drawer of his file cabinet, took out an envelope, spilled the contents onto the conference table: a couple dozen photos, mostly of faces, the photos and faces in various states and sizes, some of the photos obviously taken postmortem. He splayed out all the pictures, then began grouping and regrouping them, setting and unsetting a hierarchy in a group, sliding a whole group closer to another group. As he worked, his jaw clenched, he removed his hat, ran his fingers through his hair, replaced his hat, repeatedly. He scratched his back through his safety vest. His thousand bug eyes were having trouble maintaining focus. I signaled to my wife to observe. It appeared that this intelligence officer or contractor or whatever he was—he was never going to make much sense of the people in front of him. But he kept at it—the bureaucrat's imperative. And he was good at needling us.

Among the photos, I noticed some faces that we knew.

"Stuck in the past," he said after an interlude of shuffling pictures. "People here, people who come here, people who are sent here, who are invited here—because they can't let go of the past. You see what I'm saying?"

"Not exactly," I replied, trying to sound man-to-man confident and confidential. My wife sighed and looked away.

"Your other project, your other investigation. The thing is, those times are over. The old methods, the disappearances, long gone. This is a reform government. These guys are educated; they are articulate. They went to our schools. They're about efficiency, prosperity, getting it done."

I wanted to tell him that he was deluded or a liar, that just days before we'd been waist-deep in a mass grave that was less than a year old. But I kept quiet.

He said, "You don't like me. You don't like what I do. But you need my help. You see what we're up against here."

"I see a disaster we helped create."

"Okay, that's your theory. Now what are you going to do?" he said. "You're just an annoyance, you two."

He went back to shuffling the photos, making associations, lifting his eyebrows, then reshuffling them, like a game of deadly solitaire.

"Lie to me," he said after a bit of this.

I said nothing, not quite able to stifle my surprise, which gave him obvious pleasure.

"You called the consulate this morning," he said. "You asked them to send somebody to help you."

He paused.

"They did. The consulate. They sent me."

He ratcheted up the smile again. He was back in his zone.

"'Lie to me,'" he said. "General passcode. Beautiful, no? My idea. 'Lie to me.' Hmm? I say it to you to prove that I'm the helper they dispatched to rescue you. Aw, you look lost. Now you're lost."

He gloated for a moment, then went on.

"The time comes when you have to take action, my friends. Your passports."

We left the room, leaving our rescuer at his table. We went to the airline's customer-service counter. While we were wrangling over our tickets, we heard that we had missed that afternoon's flight out.

THE EARTH IS FLAT

No discussion, no consultation, no debate, not then. We made a break for the outside, for the taxi stand, to see how far we could get, running, as best we could, with our luggage and the oversize metal case that held the biosamples. The case rolled on wheels, but lifting it into the taxi's trunk required the assistance of the driver, and the car shuddered considerably when this burden was dropped in. The driver studied the case, studied us, and shrugged, a man resigned to the unknown. We put one of our bags into the remaining space in the trunk and took the rest with us into the backseat.

"Where to, my friends?" the driver asked as he turned down the volume of his music and pulled away from the curb. His car was highly personalized, but there was one photo we thought we recognized.

"The president?" I inquired.

"The president is in every taxi," the driver said. Then he laughed uproariously. "He has his eye on you," the driver said, and he laughed a bit more, then abruptly stopped, went quiet, then asked again, "Where to?" looking at me in the rearview mirror.

I named the free country to the north across the

border, that border being a drive of several hours from where we were.

"Oh!" the driver exclaimed. He placed his hand over the picture of the president. "Where did you say?"

I repeated it.

He kept one hand over the president's picture and his other hand left the steering wheel to gesture to us to get our ears closer to him. We did.

"You see, my friends, that border was closed two days ago, as they sometimes do." Then he gestured us closer still, and in the lowest audible voice he said, "I tried it myself just yesterday."

"Could you take us somewhere we could walk across?" I asked.

"And your case, in the back," he said. "You would leave it with me?"

"We could roll it?" I suggested.

"At the border, there is one road," the driver said. "And that road is guarded. Soldiers. Away from the road, the wheels on your case would do no good. And if you tried to carry it, you two . . ." There he took his eyes off the road to swing around and look directly at each of us in the backseat for way too long. Finally, eyes back front, he continued: "Even if you could, you two would be too easy to catch, and it, the case, too hard to hide. And then, well . . . What is in the case, if now I may ask?"

My wife started to tell me no, but I went ahead. "Bones, air, water, flowers, dust," I said.

"You have not enough of these things where you are

from?" he asked, and took the opportunity to laugh some more.

"We are investigating the death of a young boy from this country. He died in our city. These samples will help us figure out exactly where he came from."

"What does it matter?" the driver asked, no longer jovial. After a silence, he continued: "Time to think, my friends, time to decide. If you want to cross the border, you would have to leave that case behind, somewhere." He looked at me in the rearview mirror again.

My wife looked at me, too, then leaned against the door on her side of the taxi and stared out her window, for a time. Then, still leaning away, she turned only her head toward me. "You wouldn't," she said. "You wouldn't consider it, leaving the case. The evidence."

"What do you think?" I asked her.

She turned and looked out her window again. Neither of us spoke, the driver glancing at us in his rearview mirror, probing us as we sped by people at the side of the road carrying plastic bags, carrying packages tied with string, carrying buckets, carrying children, carrying nothing.

My wife conceded at last. "I think you would not," she said. "You wouldn't leave the case. I think"—here she hadn't rotated even her head in my direction—"I think my mind is poisoned," she said, gazing up now at the strange trees.

Also out there was the sharp form of a young boy, orange shorts, no shirt, no shoes, running alongside the taxi, at our speed, bumping his way through the other people, looking in through the window at me, at us, his

72   *Not Long Ago Persons Found*

head and hands out of sync with this body, water dripping behind him.

I directed my wife's attention that way. Her eyes flared a moment. Then she shook her head no. And to tell the truth, I probably hadn't seen him, either.

All the while, the driver had been watching us in his mirror with increasing concern, switching his head position to see one of us, then the other.

"Take us back," I told him finally.

"Yes, my friends, I think that is right," he said. He lifted his hand off of the picture of the president, added that hand to the other on the steering wheel, made an abrupt U-turn. He was unremittingly glum now, his eyes strictly on the road ahead; he would not look at us in the mirror.

Soon enough we were back where we'd started. As we got out of the taxi and unloaded our luggage and the samples case, a man in uniform noticed us and began to approach. The driver saw him, and at the instant that we were clear of the vehicle, the driver jumped in and sped off, without payment, leaving the man in uniform looking dumbly at the space the taxi was disappearing into. Then that man turned to us and smiled, a curious attempt at the million-dollar smile.

MR. FIX FIX

We made our deal with the devil, and he was a trickster to the end. He held up our plane tickets. The bug eyes, the smile. I reached for the envelope in his hand.

"Ah!" he said, pulling the tickets away. "Your other investigation."

We said nothing.

"Who are you working for? Who sent you?" he asked.

"Who do you work for?" I countered.

"You. I am yours." The smile. "And so?"

I shuffled my feet, looked at my wife, looked back.

"Okay," I said. I looked around, looked up to the nearest security camera, leaned in close to his ear, and gave him the name of an army general we had heard of.

My wife was perfect. Sometimes we were perfect together. The flinches on her face conveyed that our regret was deep to have to reveal it, but, yes indeed, that was the name of our other overseer.

Mr. Fix's smile weakened. I sometimes thought that behind his bug eyes he could be hallucinating. Finally, he unstalled himself and said, "Bullshit. I will verify that. Or not."

I shrugged, as if I could not help him with his doubts. I

74 *Not Long Ago Persons Found*

hoped that by the time he was able to complete his check, we would be back in our city. I hoped there would be protection for us there. But now, these years later, all the major players in this story are dead except for me and the junior officer, and I'm telling you, O future, there was no sanctuary in our city anymore.

(Though my wife is possibly still alive. I've heard that she has been seen.)

Anyway, back then, back there, the fixer did give us our tickets, and a few hours later we were in line for that afternoon's flight out. Two of their policemen watched us. A third arrived and spoke to them; then the three walked away. They were the last uniformed peace officers from that country that we saw.

We crossed the tarmac to the airplane. At the foot of the steps up stood a young man in some other uniform from the costume rack. He grinned enthusiastically when we came forward. He stretched out his hand. Into it we placed an envelope containing our passports. He slipped the envelope into his shirt pocket, where it didn't entirely fit, the top of the envelope protruding above the pocket, a small slip of the colored covers of our passports showing, for anybody to see.

"Have a nice journey," he said. He angled one hand up and planed it into the air like a great bird taking off. He made the sound of two jet engines.

"We'll try," my wife replied.

We climbed the steps, went through the door, found our seats. Two people with no verifiable identity and one piece of our luggage full of bones, dust, and air.

I remembered the name then, the Mariana Trench, the deepest point under any ocean—eleven kilometers below sea level. A deep, deep dive, at the bottom of which one continental plate is being pushed below another.

THE CITY

LANDING

We could speak the language with the accent of the city, we had an address they could go check, we could sing the national anthem, pledge allegiance to the flag, name presidents going backward through previous wars, but there was a problem with our passports: We had none. Immediately, at the airport, we were bundled off to separate interrogation rooms, windowless. Mine was furnished with a nominal desk, a chair, a guest chair, a young officer in a tan uniform, and in an upper corner, a TV monitor, the same make and model as the monitors in the interrogation rooms we'd just left.

"That stays on," the officer said when he saw me looking at the TV. "They're new," he added.

It was showing a news channel, the volume low. He picked up a remote, flipped the monitor through some views of different parts of the airport we were in. He stopped at an image of a room like this one, my wife in the guest chair, looking up at the camera in her room. Her immigration officer, essentially the same as mine, asked her a question. She didn't answer, her eyes still looking into the camera. My officer flipped our monitor back to the news.

The officer's tan uniform and lack of weapons conveyed that this windowless room could have been perched out near a remote border, surrounded by miles of open trails, and the officer could have found us and offered water and directions. Then the tan uniform was supplemented with a saturated midnight black jumpsuit on a second officer in the room, his pant legs tucked into high, thick-soled leather boots. He paced the room. We'd seen this look before. The concept was that any situation might require action and he was ready. I was a disappointment; all we did was talk. Then those two uniforms were reinforced by the crisp, pressed, blue uniform of the urban police, with a full inventory of weapons and communicators, and a badge—on a third officer in the room.

All these uniforms were probably made in the same cheap labor part of the world as the uniforms of the police and army in the country we'd just left.

The city cop turned off his radio, turned off his lapel camera, escorted me to a new room, no apparent camera, so no record of what could occur there. In that room, my wife was seated at a table with the philosopher, our principal contact at Central, who was wearing a suit, possibly made in the same factory as the uniforms, but on a different shift.

The philosopher was amused. He sent us home.

That night we transferred the contents of the top part of our biosamples case to a different case, of identical appearance but no false bottom. We transferred the contents from under the false bottom of the original case to an old piece of luggage from the storage room. At 4:00 A.M., we rolled that old suitcase out our back door, out a back gate, through a neighbor's yard, to the street, to a nearby park, to an unlighted trail, where a woman we'd met once took possession of the suitcase, rolled it left at a fork in the trail, where we went right without it, out of the park, back through the neighbor's yard, back home.

At 6:00 A.M., we loaded the new samples case—absent the hidden compartment of the previous case—into a taxi, got out one block early, rolled the case to the alley beside Central, down the alley to the loading dock. Together, we pushed and pulled the case up the side steps to the dock level. My wife punched in her code, the huge door rattled up, we pushed in to bright lights. The case was taken over by two techs, who rolled it through double doors to the freight elevator to the evidence lab. The double doors slammed shut, the loading dock door rattled down, we exited the building by the side man door, and stood on the landing, looking at each other.

"Do I know you?" my wife asked.

"Not much," I replied.

"Can we talk?" she asked.

We did talk, over breakfast, and it was better than usual, but still like ice-skating—that is, on ice over a lake, over deep water. That night, we pushed our chest of drawers over to block the bedroom door and we made love on the floor, like at the airport, before. My wife's attraction to risky behavior, reckless behavior, I've said that I shared it, but there were times when I thought this was all I'd ever get from her.

INTO THE DRAGON

Days, we worked at the evidence lab, well equipped, at Central. Evenings and weekends, we worked at the other lab, not so well equipped, with evidence from the group grave sites, the evidence we'd smuggled in under the false bottom of our samples case. Sleep, we didn't much. Then Wednesdays we were to report to the philosopher on progress in the day lab. First of those Wednesdays, my wife began:

"Let's start with where we came in: the bones. You may remember that when the body and head and hands were first brought together in the morgue, you had no idea where he was from, though you thought not from here. Normal forensics didn't tell you much. You called us. First thing, we set up to get a bone sample from him. Couldn't use his feet—not reliable, since they were found separately from the body. So a section from the femur, his thighbone."

"I was there," the philosopher said. Then he stopped himself.

I'd been there, too. Just as the saw was poised above the boy's thigh, his head had moved, rolled to one side, his mouth slightly open. We all saw it, and there was a likely rational explanation: The head, which had been severed from the torso and found separately, had been merely laid down on the body tray up against the neck, in the place the head should have been. When the head rolled, it could have been simply that it had not been secured in place, that the gurney had been jostled by one of us, that maybe the gurney wheels had not been locked.

But also, at the moment the saw was powered on, I thought I heard a sound, like a man falling into a cave, like a tree being cut, like a bird's wing being torn off, like a grass fire. My wife stopped the saw. The other sound stopped with it. I'd looked at her. She and I said nothing about it until later, and I didn't ask any of the others in the room, though it appeared we were all shaken. My wife started up the saw again. Through a gap that had been cut in the outer layers of skin, fat, and muscle, she sawed out a complete section of the femur—bone sheath, bone, and marrow. She extracted the bone section, dropped it into a large jar, folded the outer layers of the boy's thigh back closed. The body was rolled away, returned to its shelf in the banks of chilled body shelves in the morgue.

That night we'd told each other that there was surely also a rational explanation for the sound we thought we'd heard, but this incident had been the beginning of our other obsession.

"What a way to begin an investigation," the philosopher said, back to the business at hand.

My wife returned too:

"Right. So. We used maggots to clean the extraneous soft tissue off of our sawed-out sample," she said.

"You have maggots in the lab?"

"Local bait and tackle shop, down by the river. Maggots by the half liter."

She lifted one eyebrow, lowered the opposite eyelid, then continued.

"So now we had a complete clean section of a major bone, the femur. Different parts of the bone are made in different phases, as the bone grows, remodels, and repairs. In this case, at his age, we could assume that our sample included close enough to all phases, from his newest bone to his oldest. We had a bone record of his entire life, beginning to end.

"We compared the radioactive isotopes in the minerals from different parts of that record, different subsections of bone, to other parts—comparing different phases of bone formation to other phases. We also compared these bone subsections to the minerals in his teeth. Teeth, once formed, don't change much, so their mineral content is a stable marker of that time, when they were made, a cross-reference.

"You, sir, if we sampled different parts of your bones, we'd find mineral isotopes from the different places you've lived, at different times, unless you sprang up fully formed right here in this building and never left."

"I met you out at the airport," the philosopher argued.

"That wouldn't show up."

"Our subject . . . " I intervened.

"Our subject, this boy," she resumed. "Just one place. The isotope profiles from all his subsamples matched. We could conclude that his bones and teeth were built entirely from the rocks and soils, and water, and plants of a single place. He'd been in that place all his life, his short life. Until just before he came to our city.

"Okay so far?" my wife asked.

The philosopher nodded.

"Next, we brought in a geophysicist," she continued. "The isotopes in the boy's bones and teeth could also give us some idea of where in the world his single location, his place, might be. His isotopes were compared to the isotopes in specific geological formations, so we could narrow down the subject's origins to a few areas of the globe where that geological set, at this moment in the Earth's history, is at or near the surface, where minerals with those isotope profiles could get into the local humans' diet and so into their bones.

"We also cross-referenced the bone isotopes to rainfall data from the GNIP, the Global Network of Isotopes in Precipitation, since rainwater is a major source of the isotopes in bones. This and others of his isotopes gave us indications of relative altitude, proximity to seafood, food plant types, and other details.

"All put together, we could narrow the probable location of the subject's origin, his possible birthplace, to one of two or three geographic regions."

"Why not use dental records?" the philosopher asked, beginning to get restless.

"Sure, no problem, sir. We did use the mineral content of his teeth, as I said. But as for the pattern, the map of his teeth, his bite? Well, first, so far we'd reduced the scope of his possible origin from the entire globe down to a small number of nation-states, but still, a few million square miles, populated by maybe a few million people, in or near a few thousand towns, with a few thousand dentists, and we didn't have the budget to go around asking all those dentists. And, second, given the likely poverty of this boy's upbringing, there may or may not be a local dentist who may or may not have X-rays or impressions of some local children's teeth that we could match up to the teeth in the head that you found."

"Okay, okay, I get the picture."

"So that was where we were with the bones and teeth, stuck there, before you got our travel authorized."

"I remember."

"It was the pollen, which we'll get into next week, that allowed us to focus further, on a small-enough area to travel to: a single country, that one part of a river valley, between those two cities, an area where there is, in effect, only one major road, which follows the river. So the pollen directed us there, as we will see, and you got us a travel grant."

"On your guarantee."

"Right. So, to stay with the bones, our topic this week, one thing we did while we were in that country was take actual samples of rocks, soils, and water from specific places in order to analyze the isotopes from mineral materials found in situ, not just from databases. And also animal bones, from carcasses in local markets, to test their mineral content, too."

"Hence the smell of your samples case."

"Indeed. And also . . ."

Here she hesitated, looked at me, and what I saw in her eyes, not for the first time, was a shade, a specter of disturbance, another her, which, on its own, would never have survived the university and forensics training, would not be able to concentrate on her work now.

She turned away from me and picked up again.

"And also . . . also we got a couple of human bones."

"How?"

"Local morgue. Bodies they'd never identify anyway, and they didn't care about, so they let us take a bone or two."

"Wouldn't there be a taboo against that, disturbing the remains?"

"We found a guy who burned some stuff, said some words, made it right."

Bald-faced lies, as they say, and she was a skilled liar. The only human bones we had came from our unauthorized grave digging and had been stored in the secret compartment of the samples case and had been analyzed in the other lab. She was mixing our secret work into our government work, and I understood that she did so because the secret work was making her, was making both of us, increasingly angry, against our instincts for self-preservation.

"Anyway, to sum up," she told the philosopher, "the isotope signatures of the samples of minerals, water, and bones from that country, that river valley, matched up with the isotope signatures of the subject's bones. Conclusion: Our expedition verified that the victim's bone composition was consistent with an origin and an entire life somewhere along that road, near that river, under that rain. A conclusion we could not have reached until we traveled there."

"Okay, time's up. Are you watching the schedule?"
"We'll be ready with the pollen next week."
"And DNA?"
"Oh, DNA . . ."
"Okay, you can explain later."

And so we were out, still exiting, at that time, through the front door of his office. We took a break—to the street, to the park near headquarters, to a quiet part of the park that some people were afraid to venture into.

"The human bones. The other project. Do you know what you're doing?" I asked.

"No," she said.

The second Wednesday, our second report to the philosopher, my wife began:

"You remember, sir, where we were before we traveled, before the samples expedition. The minerals in the subject's thighbone section, the profile of their radioactive isotopes, had directed us to areas of the planet where his bones could have originated. A start, but still too large a geographic extent to investigate in any detail, too many people. If we wanted to go somewhere to confirm the minerals, we still didn't know where to go.

"Meanwhile, you got no missing person's report that

matched the found corpse. You announced your find, you had a press conference, nobody came forward. If he had a family anywhere reachable, they were silent.

"So, bones, his suitcase, the clothes on the corpse, the color of his skin after two days in the river. Just hints. Still, where was this boy from? What next?"

"Yes . . ." the philosopher pressed.

"Sir, you say you go out. If we sampled your clothes, we *could* track that—your movements for the last week, the last month. The places you've been. Here, at work, of course, and anywhere else."

The philosopher appeared to be unperturbed.

"And if we could get into your stomach, we'd know where you're getting your food—where it was grown, and probably what stores, what restaurants you've been to. If you were up to something, we could find out. There'd be things you couldn't hide."

She paused.

"And how?" she asked. "Pollen. There was pollen in the boy's lungs, as you heard. Also in his stomach, on his clothes, in his suitcase. And this pollen, like his thighbone, came from somewhere else."

"How long?" the philosopher asked. "How recent, before the—"

"Three to five days. He'd been in our city three to five days before he was killed. Before that, the other place."

"Will that hold up? The time frame is critical."

"Oh it is? I see. Why?" my wife asked.

"Could you make it three to five months?" the philosopher asked.

"No."

"Three to five months would be better. You're just guessing, right? The pollen."

"No. The pollen is exact. If you want to base it on evidence."

They had a stare-down. I could have told the philosopher he wouldn't get far with that.

Finally my wife said, "Okay, let's back up. Pollen. Pollen contains male sex cells, for plants that reproduce that way, plants that use flowers or seed cones, like pinecones, and so forth. Pollen is the male cells out looking for female cells to adjoin to, for those plants, of that species, to reproduce, or to migrate.

"The pollen powder that you can see, like on a bee, that's already a large quantity, a mass of pollen. To see individual grains, you need a microscope. And with an electron microscope, you can see that the outer casing of each pollen grain has marks and dents and pits that are unique to that species of plant. The pollen from the species of grass on this hill could be different from the pollen of the grass on that hill, this pine tree versus that pine tree, this river valley versus that river valley, this country that country, grass versus trees versus bushes—all unique. And exact, because of the marks on the casings. This is why pollen is exact.

"So pollen is identifiable by plant type, and the grains, the casings, can remain intact for thousands of years, and plants produce thousands, millions of them. Everything is covered with different types of pollen; the air is filled with blizzards of it, fertile, invisible—pollen riding the wind, carried by bees, hitchhiking on animal fur. The urge of plants to live, to make more of themselves—the plants' desire, their seduction. From the plants' point of view, pollen is a wide fog through which animals and humans sometimes walk.

"The result is that pollen is a universal recording device. As a person moves around, they pick up pollen grains that can be traced back to the places they've been. We're coated with our history. We eat it; we breathe it in. That five-thousand-year-old guy they found in the Alps? They used pollen to cross-check where his last meals came from."

"He was murdered," the philosopher said.

"Ambushed, that's the theory," my wife said. "An arrow to the back, then a blow to the head. Then they rolled him over onto his stomach to pull out the arrow, for later reuse. Our ancestors. They left him like that, face down. He froze, then remained there until noticed, five thousand years later, by two climbers. And then, finally, his autopsy.

"Anyway," she continued. "Another application for pollen analysis: ma—"

"Whoa," I interjected. "Focus. Our subject." I smiled like a crossing guard.

She did halt and recalibrate, but there was a moment between my wife and me, and the philosopher made note of it. I could see he was thinking this was a hook that could be used later.

"Uh-huh," he concluded. Then to my wife: "You're a strange one."

"You have no idea," she replied, glaring at me.

"So. What the pollen tells us about our subject," the philosopher prodded.

"But what the pollen hasn't told us about *our subject* is what was driving him. What did he care about? What was his goal? Did he have a mission? Was he desperate, this seven-year-old?"

"Just as to where he was from," the philosopher persisted.

"Where he was from. Right. Yes." She reset again. "Pollen in him and all over him and his things, as I said. Pollen in his lungs from the air he breathed, in his stomach from the food he ate. So first let's consider his origin, where he was from—that is, the pollen not from our city. We found grains from two tree species and a type of grass not local to here that we could reference to an international pollen database. One of the trees grows in wide swaths in a few parts of more than one continent or island."

She pulled up on her screen a world map showing three broad areas shaded in light green.

"The other tree grows in different swaths in just one area."

She added a shape of dark green to the map.

"Likewise the grass type."

She added a shape of light blue.

"And where do all three plant species intersect, where he could breathe in pollen from all three of them in the days before he traveled here? And also, where the isotope profile of the minerals in that area matches the isotope profile in his bones? Just one place. Here."

She pointed to a zone where the green and blue shadings intersected. Then she pulled out a paper map, our travel map, and pointed to a hand-marked boundary around the topographic contours of a river valley—the river, the flats above, the terraces above that.

"Here. This country, where we went, between the capital city on the coast and this regional capital inland, in the valley along this river, and the one road, the A121, that parallels the river, connecting the two cities. That is the one and only area of the world that he could have come from, where the three types of pollen and those bone-making minerals are all present. That was the hypothesis."

"And that's where we paid for your travel to," the philosopher said.

"Exactly. To collect biological samples, to show the boy's picture around, to ask questions. To test the hypothesis of that general area, to try to identify a more specific locus within it, if we could, and, at the outside, to find his family, his mother or a relative, or anyone who had just seen the boy around."

"So, two months, a salary—two salaries—expenses. And what do we have?"

"Partial success."

"Oh joy."

"Right. Based on pollen from the boy's body and possessions, compared to pollen from the country we traveled to, contrasted to pollen from around our city, we can say the following with a high degree of confidence. He was certainly from close by that river, along that road, the A121—because of matching pollen we gathered in place there from the trees and grasses, just as we had mapped them in advance. And also, from our fieldwork, we got a match to a corn pollen from around one specific town. That corn pollen is heavy; it doesn't travel far in the wind. So that's his town, or near it. Here, Township C."

She tapped her finger on a dot on our travel map.

"Furthermore, in that town we had a find, human intelligence. A couple of leads in response to the boy's picture that we were showing around. People talked to us. As we told you earlier, and we will go into details when we have time, further down the line.

"And next, had he been anywhere else on his way here? Probably a number of days, up to a few weeks, in a slightly different environment, possibly the capital city, where his river ran to the coast."

She tapped on the paper map again.

"And next, how long had he been in our city? Three or four days, maximum five, because . . ." She paused, looked up at the philosopher, then continued. "Because there was pollen at the bottom of his intestines that had to be from his home country, but in the middle it was food from around our city, though not much of it. So there's your three to five days. The pollen types are exact, and that's the timing of food through the digestive tract, like a clock. Can't be faked."

"Okay. We'll see. Maybe there's a work-around," the philosopher said calmly.

"The time frame is whether this boy was in his country when certain events occurred there, before he came here?"

"Let's stick to just this individual. Please proceed."

"Mm-*hmm* . . . So," my wife continued. "Another implication: The short time between his home food and food from our city, to get here that fast, he had to fly."

"A boy that age?"

"Yes, sir."

"Alone?"

"We don't know. But the building where you found the head and the other items, the suitcase, the building was empty, right? Nobody. We assume he was there alone until he was killed."

"A boy that age came through our airport unaccompanied? Nobody stopped him? Nobody helped him?"

"Sir, today, that is possible," she said.

"The airport cameras?" the philosopher asked.

"Precisely," I said. "Based on the pollen in his digestive tract, plus an estimate of how long his body had been in our river, we had a seventy-two-hour interval for his likely arrival by plane. We requested the security videos from the airport for that time frame. That's many hours and many cameras, at least the ones that are working. They sent over an entire hard drive with the data. We sent that to the facial-recognition contractor. The contractor sent back images of masks and large dolls from gift kiosks around the airport. Maybe because the model they were trying to match was the boy's dead face on his head drained of blood, as you found it.

94   *Not Long Ago Persons Found*

"So we asked them to do suitcase recognition. They asked did we know that suitcases are not faces. I said yes, we did. Then they got to it and found a few suitcases of the same size and shape as the boy's, but only a couple with the shade of blue that matched the suitcase found in the building where it is presumed he had been sleeping at night. And from the video intervals with suitcase matches, we were able to extract two stills of our young male subject, two images that are certainly him when he arrived at our airport."

I placed two glossy printouts on the desk, pointed to one.

"This one shows him from the front. Is he searching for somebody? We can't tell. This other one shows him from behind, as he's on his way out, a very small boy, pulling his suitcase behind him, pushing out one of the doors from the terminal interior to the arrivals apron outside. Where is he going? We don't know. There doesn't seem to be anybody around him. He is alone, leaving the airport alone. That door he's going through leads to the public buses going into the city. See, there, the sign above the door. You can see part of it."

"That's it? Two images?" the philosopher asked.

"The contractor said we burned up their computer."

"There could be more?"

"Maybe, but they won't talk to us now. We'd like to look for another contractor, but we are required to sub this out to them."

"So they know somebody," the philosopher said. "All right, let's get back to the stomach contents."

"Yes," my wife said. "Now, sad to say, the boy had had almost nothing to eat for a full day before he died."

Here my wife looked at me, a troubled look again.

"Oh," the philosopher said. He was distracted. He was looking at the TV monitor in the upper corner of his office. A body was being carried out of an empty building. This was followed by stock footage from an auto factory, stock footage of people on a city sidewalk. Without the voice-over, we had no idea how that all fit together. Then the philosopher's attention returned to us.

"And the beans?" he asked.

My wife continued to look at me, her unease transitioning to calculation.

"The beans?" she echoed.

"Beans and some other stuff, gold flakes, some kind of potion," the philosopher said.

"Yes, sir, there were beans in his stomach, partially digested just before he died, and some other material. There's something fishy about that mix—sorry, something suspicious. We'll get back to you about it."

"Maybe some kind of ritual."

"Possibly. We'll get back to you."

And that was the end of that Wednesday report. We went out, still through the front door of his office, out of the building, to the park, to the dangerous part of the park. It was late, late afternoon.

"Who are you in this?" my wife asked me.

"I had to stop you," I countered. "I could see it in your

96   *Not Long Ago Persons Found*

face. Back there, about pollen, you were going to bring up graves—mass graves, our mass graves. But you can't. Not around him. Not even a hint."

"The pollen will tell us what happened."

"Yes—"

"Did they all die in the same place at the same time? Did they die where they were buried?"

"But—"

"Were they civilians, farmers? And the season, the time of year they were killed—"

"Yes, but—"

"Were the bodies from a group grave dug up and scattered to smaller graves to conceal the crime?"

"Yes, but you can't talk about it there. No graves, not any. Not in that building. They're already suspicious of us, of what else we're up to. We can't—"

"Hold it." She stepped in front of me, poked my chest, grabbed my shirt at the collar. "Those people, they have to know the day will come when they can't hide. They won't get away with it. The evidence will speak. And the sooner they know that, the better. It will make them stop. Some of them."

We had been walking fast, oblivious, and now didn't recognize the part of the park we'd got to. The path looked to be headed into the river. Not so funny we'd picked that route.

We were locked there for a moment; then I said, "Back this way, I think," and we reversed, arriving at a cross-path we were pretty sure was on our mental map. In that location, my wife asked me if I'd told the philosopher about the beans.

"No," I said.

"Well, I didn't tell him," she stated. Which leaves what?

"Why would it have been me who told him?" I asked. "Why would I do that? When?"

She didn't answer.

We were off again, same fast pace.

"Was it in the autopsy report?" I suggested.

"Not clearly. And I doubt he read the autopsy."

"Or he has some other reason to know," I speculated. "Someone higher in the building or outside the building knows about the beans and told him."

"Or you told him."

"But I didn't."

We continued, at breakneck speed for pedestrians, until, slowing us down finally, she said, "So. It *appears* . . . we have someone in our lab at headquarters who has their own ideas, and is reporting to the philosopher directly. A spy.

"And the beans," she went on, "because we might have a spy . . ." She stopped and scrutinized me again. "We need to get some of the beans and that admixture out of there, over to our other lab. There's something not right about them."

Then we started toward home, normal pace, breathing our share of pollen, leaving our tracks in the dust.

✳

That night I noticed our cat watching me from afar, his deep green eyes cool assessors in his black face, observing, as cats do, but this was different, and why me? He'd been with us for two years, that cat, since he'd invited himself in one cold night, and he'd been grateful and devoted to us both, and he'd been happy to see both of us when we returned from our travels, but now there he was on the bookshelf, or in a corner, looking up from cleaning his paws, cleaning his chest, stopping to stare at me, more than curious, looking deep into me, jumping down and walking away casually when I approached.

I assured the damn cat I wasn't the spy in the lab, but he knew nothing about that, so he wasn't appeased. It was something else about me that he was noticing.

The third Wednesday was supposed to start with the DNA. My wife told the philosopher that the DNA might be a dead end because we had a general match between the boy and ethnic groups that had historically inhabited that river valley, but otherwise no relatives had come forth, nor been discovered, to test a specific DNA link. So the boy's identity might still be out of reach.

"No family at all," the philosopher said.

"None," she confirmed.

Then she slowly turned her eyes from the philosopher to me, and what I saw in there this time was a watchdog at a wire fence at night, head down, dripping in the rain. Then she looked back to our boss.

"None living," she said.

We'd set a computer at our other lab to run comparisons of the boy's DNA, sequenced for us officially, to DNA from bodies in the graves on the terraces, DNA that had been sequenced for us unofficially. And when we'd returned, hours later, that computer was dinging softly, like a warning that a stranger was approaching, and on the computer's screen, a red highlight bar was across one of the rows of one of the data tables. My wife called me over.

"We have a match," she said.

"Those are the boy's people; that is his valley," I said.

"No, a match to fifty percent of his DNA. The grave of forty plus three. Body number seventeen, female. He shares half his DNA with her."

"Half his DNA, meaning . . ."

"That's his mother."

"Oh. So. The church gift shop clerk, that's what he said. That she's dead."

"Yes."

"So. Killed. Recently."

"Yes."

We'd made this discovery just the day before. Still, it was another thing we ought to have shut up about for the time being, but my wife did not. "None living," she'd said to the philosopher.

"Hmm?" he asked.

"There might be a match to a female who is dead," she said.

"A dead female found where?" he asked. He paused, then repeated, "Where did you find the female match?"

"The morgue," my wife said. "In that town. Where we had the contacts."

"Is that so?" the philosopher asked. "What's the probability of that? Testing corpses in the morgue, finding a match?"

We kept quiet, now in retreat.

"You two," he went on. "What were you doing down there? The whole story."

"Just as we've said," my wife replied.

"You know we have assets there."

"Of course," my wife said.

"Of course," I said.

The philosopher opened the drawer of his desk, pulled out a manila envelope, pulled from that a single sheet of paper, and laid it on his desk in front of us. It was the page with the points, slices, loops, and off-lines that my wife and the junior officer had made while they were discussing pollen and spore and mineral isotopes and the river biome, and how to use such evidence. The philosopher turned the sheet sideways, then a 180, then twisted his head to a diagonal view, then back again.

"What's this?" he asked.

"Just doodles while we were talking," my wife said. "Me and a policeman there."

"I'll send it to Code; they'll figure it out," the philosopher said, placing the sheet of paper on top of his scanner.

"Could we focus now on the beans, if you're going to do us any good," he said.

"Noted," my wife said. She put away the DNA file and took out her file labeled "Beans Plus."

"In the boy's stomach, partially digested," she began, "a quantity of small beans, together with an odd mix of other materials, organic and inorganic, that we are still—"

"Flakes of gold, rare earths, bone splinters, other stuff. A potion. A black-magic potion," the philosopher said.

"Perhaps. We are investigating. In any case, the beans and the additives were virtually alone in his stomach, as he'd had almost nothing to eat for a day. Perhaps deliberately starved."

"Yes. Yes. And the purpose?" he asked.

"Sir, do you have children?"

"Grown. You?"

"Not likely. Not likely now."

She glanced sideways at me, then went on.

"As for the beans, they were partially digested, so we can assume they had released some active ingredients into the body. Sir, these beans are poisonous. It is claimed that they are used to paralyze a victim, for a . . . taking, a ritual taking. Typically it would be an animal, but there are reports, or rumors, of their use on humans. The poison keeps the victim alive, conscious, heart beating, aware but incapable of action, up to the moment of death—his throat cut, his head detached. Then the hands and feet. The objective of this procedure, with the beans, being to maximize the flow of blood from the body during the . . . during the killing."

"The sacrifice."

"If you will. We can assume this boy was conscious

and saw someone approach him with a knife, approach his throat, but he couldn't move. Your worst nightmare. His last brain activity, his last image of the universe. In our city."

"A ritual sacrifice, black magic, the potion, someone from his country," the philosopher said. He was smiling—a bad sign.

"Maybe. As we told you, there's something suspicious about that mix," my wife said.

"Oh?" The philosopher did not want his balloon to be punctured.

"We've got a contact in that country on this subject. We'll ask him," my wife said.

"Who's your contact?"

"We'll go to him directly."

"Your black-magic expert. We'd like to know who he is."

"It's in my other notes."

"Okay, well, then you should—"

"This concoction, the beans," my wife interrupted. "We will analyze it more thoroughly."

"Okay, but you don't have forever. We're looking to wrap this up. I think the end is near, so to speak."

Out of his office, still by the front door, out of the building, to the park, to the dangerous part, where one could be robbed—"the path of plunder," we called it, "the corridor of opportunity." Our place to debrief.

"And now the DNA match," I said. "Too soon. I'm

telling you, when you bring in evidence from the other lab now, you're putting other people at risk; you're jeopardizing the other project."

"I'd like to break his nose," she said.

"So would I, but—"

"So arrogant, so complacent. All of them. They have no idea what's going on down there."

"Or they do, they know exactly, or think they know. In any case, we have a plan," I said.

"Oh right."

"We're going to hang them with science," I said.

We stopped moving. We had survived the violent country together, and now my wife said, "No. You two are going to sell me out."

"Which two?"

"You and the philosopher."

"Not a chance."

She looked at me, long, hard, accusatory; then she walked away, at speed.

"How can you doubt me?" I asked after her, and I took a few steps in pursuit.

She spun around and pointed at me. I stepped back.

"Get. Outta here," she said.

Then she whirled and took off again, and I let her go, alone and fast down the path. I watched as the form of my wife disappeared into the trees. A mugger would have to be quick.

She was sitting on our porch when I got there. I pushed one of the potted plants off the low side wall. It fell to the pavement below. I sat in its place. She looked at me like a wild animal with its neck in a noose. I knew that there was no reason, that there was a part of her I could never reach. One of the few things she'd ever told me about her past was that one night she was climbing down the iced outside of a parking structure, in a frigid wind, climbing down from the roof level with two other people while an unmarked police car circled up the inside toward the top, and when she was just partway down, still high enough, she understood she could decide to fall. She'd stopped climbing.

But she didn't fall, did she? Not then.

I waited. She seemed to calm a little. "Okay," I said, "where are you now?"

"Hanging on," she replied. Then she stood up to go inside. "So. We stick to the plan," she said. "Science."

We went in, where the cat was again observing me, trying harder to stay out of my way. I told the cat he had it wrong, that between my wife and me, I was the stable one.

We did, we tried to stick to the plan.

The next evening, after a long day at the headquarters lab, we waited for the techs to leave, we waited for the lights to shut off, and, to keep the lights off, I broke the motion detector. My wife asked if I couldn't have just deactivated the detector. I replied that it was deactivated because it was broken. Collateral light from the city outside fell in through the windows, not sufficient for those cheap security cameras to see much. We opened the freezer, took out a vial that contained the beans and other material that had been found in the subject's stomach. We tapped a fraction of the beans and mixture into one small plastic bag, which my wife hid under her sweater, and another fraction into another bag, which I hid in my sock.

She said that if we were caught, she would, by accidental hints and glances, direct them to my socks, so her stash would go untouched, right?

I accepted.

We made it to the other lab without incident, and started some preliminary work on the beans straight away. It took us to well past midnight. They say if you don't sleep enough, you don't dream enough, and if you don't dream enough, you break down. That's the basis for sleep deprivation as a method of so-called inquiry.

The next morning, early, we got a call to go to headquarters immediately. It was me that remembered to put down food for the cat on our way out.

When we arrived, we were directed to an observation closet with a one-way mirror looking into an interrogation room, where the philosopher sat at a table, across from a young man wearing all black, including a black band holding the base of his ponytail. Oh and one earring, a simple small flat loop of a metal too expensive to be shiny. Left ear, beside an absolutely untroubled face.

106   *Not Long Ago Persons Found*

The young man was leaning back. The philosopher was leaning forward.

". . . because, as I told the other guy, I heard your announcement, your request for help," the man in black was saying. "I thought this might be of interest."

On the table between them was a clay bottle, the height of a beer can, and on the side that we could see, on a flattened oval, was a profile of a bird's head, in solid white glaze against the natural clay background. We assumed that on the other side of the bottle was the same bird's head profile, but in black. Exactly like the bottle that the gift shop clerk in Township C had showed us, exactly what he'd told us to look for. This bottle, the one on the table in the interrogation room, was open, no cork, no top.

"Whom did you acquire it from?" the philosopher asked.

"Don't know, wasn't me that made the loan."

"The clerk on duty?"

"He might remember."

"Name of the clerk?"

"We let him go."

"But his name?"

"I don't remember."

"You could look it up."

"We have a lot of turnover. Anyway, it would just be the name he gave us."

"Why'd you let him go?"

"We were told to."

"By whom?"

"I can't say."

"You're not cooperating."

"Was that a question?"

"Look, no matter what you call your establishment, your operation, it's just a pawnshop."

"That's what we call it, a pawnshop."

"We can make things difficult for you," the philosopher said.

"That's why I'm here, to fix it so you don't. We volunteer this bottle. And you, you should ask around, your colleagues. How we have been useful in the past, the good we can continue to do for you."

The man in black was enjoying himself. The philosopher looked lost; he paused, perhaps hoping that in the silence, the dark weight of the building would bear down on the upstart across from him.

My wife whispered something to one of the policemen in our observation closet. That policeman went out into the corridor, knocked, entered the interrogation room, whispered at length to the philosopher. The philosopher looked at the bottle, pulled up the paper tag tied with a string to the bottle's neck.

"The code on this tag keys to your records, your required records," the philosopher said.

"Yes," the man in black agreed.

"Date and time that the clerk, whoever he was, took in the bottle. And the clerk's name."

"Yes. The clerk's name at the time."

"You have at least one camera in the front of your shop, the public area."

108   *Not Long Ago Persons Found*

"Yes."

"You keep the videos, as required. You hold them for the months required."

"Yes."

"You can bring us the video files for the time of the transaction, the time your shop bought the bottle."

"Yes."

"A half hour before and a half hour after. We want to see who was in the room around the exact time."

"How could I say no?"

"You can't."

The philosopher turned in his seat to look at the one-way mirror, as if he was trying to figure out who had come up with this good idea. He should have known it was her, my wife, the mistress of physical evidence, to whom most everything else was a mystery.

The philosopher turned back. "All right, then," he said.

"All right, then," the pawnshop owner said.

They paused.

"Do that," the philosopher said.

The man in black plopped his hands onto the desk, palms parallel and sideways, like two karate chops. His wrists were cuffed together by plastic loops, the excess length of the plastic ties springing in the air like termite antennae.

"Oh yeah," the philosopher said. He patted his pockets, started to go through the drawers of the desk. "That wasn't really necessary," he said. Finally, he turned again to the one-way mirror, which summoned a policeman to come into the interrogation room and cut the plastic cuffs off the wrists of the man in black. The policeman used ordinary home garden stem clippers.

The pawnshop owner left. The rest of us convened in the corridor. The philosopher looked at me, looked at my wife.

"The brain," he said to her. "That's why we called you."

He held up the clay bottle.

"Of interest?" he asked.

"Definitely," we said together.

"This would have been to carry the potion, the beans, the poison, for the sacrifice," the philosopher said.

He looked at the bird's-head profiles on the two sides of the bottle, one black, one white, each bird with a sharp beak and a predator's eye.

"Looks like an eagle," the philosopher said.

There was a silence. The bird considered us.

"I don't think they have eagles there, where the victim is from," a policeman said.

"Maybe a vulture," another policeman said.

"An osprey—they hunt in water, dive from above." That was my wife.

I looked it up later. Any one of them could have been right.

We dropped everything that day in the lab to begin analysis of the bottle.

The mineral isotopes in the clay matched those in

the boy's river valley, around Township C. Assays and bioassays of a scraping from the bottle's interior allowed us to identify its previous contents: H_2O, with traces of soils, plant debris, fish DNA, and the detritus of aquatic life typical of a body of fresh water with a consistent one-directional current. In other words, river water. It must have belonged to the boy. He had arrived in our city with a bottle of river water.

"As the church shop clerk told us. A gift from home," I said. "Or for his protection."

"Or just to talk to," my wife said.

A few days later, the video arrived from the pawnshop, delivered personally by the owner, the man in black. As he handed the envelope over to my wife, there was a charge there, on his side, an ignition. I understood it well; she had that effect. But listen, pal, you don't understand what else goes along with that.

As for my wife, maybe I shouldn't have been surprised, but what I observed, on her side, was that she knew this guy, either by type or specifically, apart from his interview at headquarters.

He left. We plugged the video he'd brought into the big monitor in the upper corner of our lab, momentarily blocking out the news feed. And what did we see?

A camera view from a high corner at the front of the shop, a fish-eye lens, exactly what a fish would observe if floating near the ceiling to one side of a pawnshop interior. And in the corner opposite the camera, their own big TV monitor. Scan-line images from the national news feed on that monitor were visible in the capture from the security camera.

Opposite the ceiling camera and monitor, down below, was the transaction counter, an idle clerk visible behind a thick plexiglass window, probably bulletproof. Beside that, a locked plexiglass portal through which larger objects of value could pass, in exchange for cash pushed out through the slot at the bottom of the clerk's window. Around the room, clean glass display cases with the things that had passed through the fateful portal or slot and had not been reclaimed: the musical instruments, amplifiers, necklaces, watches, electronics, and dining room porcelain and silver that people had abandoned there, on their way to some other world. If you wanted to equip a marching band, a polka band, a rock-and-roll mash-up, a new marriage, this would be an economical place to start. But from the other side, from the view of a person entering there to sell something, this was a ring of hell.

Daylight filtered in from the street windows behind the camera; the electric lights were off, to economize. The video, to economize, to reduce digital storage size, was at a granular resolution, with pale colors, and in stop-action mode—the one hour of real time that had been requisitioned was hacked into fifteen minutes of skippy freeze frames in video time.

At the center of the video sequence that we had was the moment of record that the bottle with the two birds on it had been received by the now not findable clerk. At the start of our viewing, nobody visible in the shop but the clerk; then the video brightens to nearly all white as the door to the street opens and daylight sluices in. The camera adjusts, then cuts to nearly black when the door is closed. When the camera adjusts again, the stop-action mode catches a customer in the room, looking around, then leaving—video to white when the door opens, to black when it closes, camera adjustment, empty shop. Another customer comes and goes, the same herky-jerky, like a fast-motion record of night wildlife at a water hole.

Five real-time minutes before the moment of the critical transaction, the room washes white, black, the camera adjusts, and a man is in the shop: exotic, dark, a strange hat, a raggedy shoulder bag. He goes to the transaction window, his back to the camera. He swings the shoulder bag around in front of him. Does he reach into it for something to show the clerk? He becomes agitated. The clay bottle, if he had it, was not too big to fit through the slot at the bottom of the plexiglass shield.

But we were not going to see the actual exchange, the bottle pushed in, the cash and claim ticket pushed out. The pawnshop owner had chosen the angle of his required public camera cleverly. We were only going to see the back of the seller, and we'd have to guess when the physical pass-through took place. We had the time of the bottle transaction, but only to the minute. For any one freeze frame within that minute, we could only guess if that was the moment of the handover.

If that was the moment, and if that was the person. Because shortly after the dark man is at the cash window, becomes agitated, and pops out a meter away, flash white, flash black, camera adjustment, then a white man is also in the shop: blond, ponytail, long coat, boots, pale as a maggot. He looks like a junkie, of local origin, but living in a different era in his head. Then this white man is at the transaction window. Does he reach for something under his coat? Then he is agitated; then he is a meter away from the counter.

The video we were watching had a date and time stamp at the bottom. As we approach the critical minute, when the clay bottle will be actually logged in, the dark man and the white man circle the room, caught looking into the display cases, caught standing again at the transaction counter, caught posturing, gesturing to the clerk, caught moving away but not leaving.

In the one minute, the sixty seconds, during which the clay bottle had been finally handed over, both men are at the exchange window twice, then return to prowling the room, satisfied or not satisfied, each wary of the presence of the other. Several minutes after the bottle has been given up, they are both still in the shop. Then the video washes to white, to black, to normal, and the white man is gone. Minutes later, the same, and the dark man is gone.

In the remaining minutes of the video record that we had, nothing—the clerk behind the window in various poses of boredom and annoyance, the shop floor empty, as if after a neutron bomb.

Had some other additional small to medium-size object been pawned in the same sixty seconds as the clay bottle purchase? We could ask the owner to check, but it wouldn't matter much. The point was, we'd seen the moment, or close, that the bottle had been sold, but we didn't know which moment it was, which person it was— the white man (the junkie) or the dark man (the exotic). We could fast forward and fast back, or slow forward and back, zoom in, zoom out, creating a macabre dance of the two men around each other and around the cash window, but we could not zero in any closer to the precise moment that one of them sold the bottle.

We did know that it was probably one of those two men who had poisoned and dismembered the boy found in our river, and it was certainly one of those two who had, after the killing, lifted the clay bottle from the scene and pawned it for a trivial sum of cash. Who had emptied the bottle of its river water, and when, we did not know.

EVERY MAN A THEORIST

At the next meeting, the philosopher said we were ready to wrap this up.

"We are?" I asked.

"The money, the time, your little vacation. We need a result," he said.

We had no comment.

"You can fill in the details later. This case is a ritual killing, a human sacrifice. The poison beans in the potion in the ceremonial bottle to paralyze the victim, the prescribed slitting of the throat, the body drained of blood for use elsewhere, the corpse dumped into moving water—our river—three tides and it's out to sea. The head to be burned—that's why it was at the furnace. The hands to be scattered at great distance—that's why they were on the roof. He was going to drop them onto a passing truck. Just like in . . . Just like in . . . Anyway, sacrifice of a human, a child, more power than sacrifice of an animal. The boy has—he had an uncle here, in this city. We're looking for the uncle. We say it's the guy in the pawnshop video, the foreigner, the immigrant—"

"The man with the hat," my wife offered.

"Him. That's the uncle. And said uncle sacrificed the

115

116   *Not Long Ago Persons Found*

boy to bring him success here, or money, or to win some dispute. Simple, clear, obvious."

"Maybe too obvious," my wife said.

"Okay, okay. The scientist, the skeptic. But we're past that. We've got an expert, and we're looking for yours." He gave us a sharp look, then continued. "They've got it figured out, see? Black magic, superstition, the poor victim, he saw it coming, et cetera, et cetera. These people are their own worst enemies."

"Who? Who has it figured out?" my wife asked.

"What floor are we on? My office?"

"Five," she said.

"How many floors in this building?"

"Twelve."

"So you, scientist, that's how many floors above me?"

"We get your point."

"And other buildings. Intelligent, interested people, in many offices, with big views."

"We get your point, we get your point."

"Our main guy on the ground there, in-country, in the victim's country of origin . . ."

"Agency?" I asked.

"Private contractor."

My wife and I looked at each other. The private contractor was certainly the fixer, the man who got us on a plane home, the man who took our passports.

"Our guy, our asset," the philosopher continued, "he went to the town. He identified your specialist, the black-magic specialist. A clerk at a gift shop in a church?"

He looked at us. We were neutral.

"That clerk will tell us what we need to know. When we find him. He's not always available, they say. But someone will tell us where he is. Or someone like him. And he will tell us what we need."

"Which is what?"

"As we said. The boy was killed by a man from his home country. Probably his uncle, who is here, in this city. A sacrifice to give the uncle the upper hand in a dispute with his landlord, let's say, over the rent, a year's back rent. Or the uncle is a human trafficker and the sacrifice will give him the power to evade the authorities."

"So you're sure what the clerk will say when you find him?"

"Ha-ha, yes. We have our ways, don't we? Now? Gloves off? To get information?"

That did shut us up for a moment.

But then my wife said, "Okay, hold on. Let's look at this. The body dumped upriver so it would take three days to float to salt water?"

"Yeah?"

"Was that deliberate? There's access to the river closer to the end, where just one tide—so a day at the most—would carry the body out to sea, undiscovered and undisturbed. If *that* was what you wanted."

"So?"

"Or they could have weighted the body to sink. It would stay down where they dumped it."

"So?"

"What do you think? And also, the head left by a furnace that wasn't working, that hadn't been working for a couple of years. And the hands, on the roof, in an empty hamburger bag? Was that a joke?"

"He had a plan; he was interrupted," the philosopher said.

"Or he was confused and/or incompetent," my wife said. "A disordered mind. Not a practitioner of the dark arts. Or he's none of that; he had a different purpose, which we don't see because we're looking at it wrong."

"Details."

"Okay. How about this? There's another lead, an individual, a shop owner, in that town. Also his wife. They may know the victim's mother. They may have sold the suitcase to her. The suitcase that was found in the building where the head and hands were found."

"Not relevant, not anymore," the philosopher said. "We say the mother sold the boy for the sacrifice. Or she could pretend she didn't know what it was for. But she needed the money. For her other children. That sounds right. They're dirt-poor. So the suitcase is a sideshow. We're looking for the church gift shop clerk. When we find him, or someone like him, we will make him talk. Simple. The uncle here has disappeared, too; we'll announce we're looking for him. So we're busy with the next phase, moving on."

He continued: "I'm working on a press release. How does this sound?" He read to us: "'The body of a young boy, an illegal immigrant, recently found in our city, pollen still in his lungs from a distant river valley, his home, a river that flows through a violent country, a country of superstition and greed . . .' uh-huh, and so on. You get it, do you not?"

He looked at us; we shrugged.

"It's a shame, isn't it?" he said. "A reform government there that we support. A strong leader. But the people, still backward."

We shrugged again.

"I expected no less from you two," he said. "So we're going to reduce your security clearance. We won't need your services much longer, to tell the truth. We'll take it from here. We would have wanted flexibility, team play. But we anticipate that you are not capable of it. From here forward, I'm going to have to ask you to come and go by the back door. Frankly, I need to disassociate myself."

We were silent again.

"Okay, then, let's do this. Opossum," he said.

The lights in his office dimmed; the volume of his TV monitor was raised.

"No," he said.

The lights went back up, the TV volume back down.

"O—po—ssssuuummmm," he said.

The wall panel that his minibar was placed against rotated slowly a quarter turn, admitting into his office a view of a stair landing outside, and the sound of a large empty vertical interior volume out there, someone talking far down or up in it.

He tipped his head toward the opening in his wall.

"The only doors your code will open now will be the entry door at the bottom of that stair and the entry door of your lab. On your way out, look at my door. Next time we meet, you'll come up the back stair, knock at that door."

We went out to the landing.

"Newt," he said.

The overhead lights in his office slithered to red, the TV volume shut off, music came on.

"No," he said.

The lights, TV, and sound reset.

"Nnnn—ewwwww—ttt," he said.

The wall panel rotated shut, leaving us alone on the landing. We noted the building coordinates stenciled on the wall above the several doors in front of us: quadrant, floor, office group numbers. Most of those doors led to corridors of other doors to other department offices. On the philosopher's private door, the title had been painted over and restenciled a few times. Currently it read OFFICE OF CIRCUMLOCUTION.

The landing we stood on was hollow-plate steel, the stair steps were an open steel mesh, and the whole assembly, welded and bolted, repeated floor by floor, above us and below us, in a unified structure within the tall stairwell silo, all the way from the low subbasements to the higher powers on top. A light fixture one level below us zapped and popped. A thick bunch of color-coded cables and wires were strapped together onto a vertical of the stair structure, one cluster of cables entering and exiting at each floor level, through a porthole. We noted three cables at this level that had sproinged out of their bundling, cut ends dangling off, waving in the air. Data spilled out from them, or data came into them from the void we were in.

We started down, our footfalls like thumps on an enormous drum in the empty twelve-floor height, plus subbasements. Reverb, latency. Some lowly architect, assigned to do the back stairs, had created a doomsday percussion chamber. As we descended, we began to coordinate our rhythm, my two steps, her two steps, drumming, for and against, my wife and I, sometimes in sync like this, as good as talking.

Three floors down, we noticed the door to the metro investigators' office. My wife tried the lock; her code had not yet been canceled. We went in, queried the receptionist, and were directed to the desk of the detective who first caught the boy's case—the headless, handless, footless juvenile corpse found in the river.

We waited. On the TV monitor above the detectives' area we saw a large swimming pool with a lone swimmer; cargo being loaded onto a military plane; a man facedown on a street, encircled by five police cars; a crowd of people on a sidewalk, flattened by a telephoto lens; a truck full of bullet holes; a man running between trees, a policeman shooting at him.

Then the detective dragged in. Introductions. He told us that a few weeks in, when still nobody had come forth to claim the body, the boy was still alone, and they had no idea where he'd come from, he and the staff decided that they had to be the boy's family. They filled out the forms. They legally adopted him.

"And we gave him a name, the boy, this young man, so he wouldn't be just a case number," the detective said.

"Nobody upstairs told us. What name did you give him?" I asked.

"Adam."

"Adam," my wife repeated.

Then there was a silence. Then the detective said, "So you're the diggers."

"Sorry?" I replied.

"You two did the field trip, to the country of interest."

"Yes."

We didn't know how much he might know about . . . about all of it.

"Curious thing," he told us. "When we found the building, the empty apartments, where the head and hands were, the suitcase, we also found a library card. The city library. Three to five days in our city you say—"

"Yes, but how did you—"

"We get transcripts of your meetings. With your supervisor. Three to five days in our city, as you say, sleeping in an abandoned building, starving, he got himself a library card."

"At that age?" I asked.

"We found the librarians," the detective said. "They remembered him. He came in wide-eyed; they showed him around, asked if he wanted to take books home, said they could issue him a library card. 'Home?' he'd asked. Now we know what he meant. But, yes, could he get a card, please. They waived proof of residence."

"And the name? The name on the card?" my wife asked.

"Bart Simpson," he said. "False of course. Covering his tracks. Clever young man."

"And frightened."

"For sure."

"But Bart Simpson?" I said. "They let him?"

"Oh, you know librarians; they're not the police."

"Where's the card now?" my wife asked.

"I suppose in the evidence room. I don't know. They told us yesterday we're off the case. They moved it to a different team. You know anything about that?"

"We're being pushed out, too," I said.

"So . . ." the detective started, stopped, started again. "A seven-year-old boy. What are we if we let this go?"

We all stood up. He turned to escort us out the front door. We steered him toward the back. He gave us a curious look. We exited onto the stair landing, drummed our way down the remaining floors to street level, then continued two more levels down and stopped to look at the door there, which led to the cold room, which was where the boy's reassembled body was being stored.

Adam.

Then we went back up to street level, the loading dock, the rolling door, the side man door, through which we exited into the alley beside the building. Then down the alley to the street.

THE ROOF

From our roof, depending on wind direction and atmospheric conditions, we could sometimes hear and see jets in the middle part of their climb out from our city, or at the decision point of their descent. Any incoming plane could be carrying another refugee, landing here with no place to go, with no plan but to stay alive. Look anywhere, you might see one, added to our own homeless, the haunts, the dispossessed. There were already so many at that time.

We were lying on the roof at dusk that evening because our other lab was in overtime for one of their legitimate contracts, because we thought if we could relax we might be able to sleep, and because the cat was sometimes happy when the three of us stretched out together up there.

"I'm sorry, but I can't not think about it," my wife said. "Adam. He came alone to our city, pollen from his home still in his lungs, a bottle of river water in his suitcase. He got himself through our airport, into downtown. He found an abandoned building to sleep in. At that age. He got himself a library card. Then somebody in our city separated his head and hands and feet from his body. And now we've reassembled him, put him back together, put him in cold storage. And he's stranded there. And that's it? That's the end of him? Nothing more?"

"What do you expect? Normal now," I said, tired.

The cat was lying on my wife's side, still partial to her, still avoiding me.

After some silence, I said, "I'm just wondering. The boy, alone, at night, in that building, did he dream of the water he would end up in? Like a bird that dreams of the gun that will shoot him."

"Mm," she said. Then, after another interval: "I had a dream."

"Uh-oh," I said, as I always did, and she went on.

"First just black water. Then floating in it, the boy's body, the parts of it back together, with labels and arrows to points of evidence, all of this just under the surface, like half-sunk leaves. Then from below, deep water, a shape comes up. A woman's head, hair out of control, wild eyes, mouth moving. The woman's head seizes the boy's arm between its teeth, her head as big as a great white shark. She pulls the boy back down with her, way down; they disappear. Then, just dark. And the sound of air bubbling out, underwater."

"Uh-huh," I said. And, after some consideration: "Well, there's a bit of that, isn't there? Could be me."

"You could be the boy in the dream?"

"Or the woman."

"No. The woman is me."

I turned on my side to look at her. "But, strictly speaking, according to the theory of dreams . . ." I began, but stopped. I could hear the cat purring, pressed against her.

Then she started again. "Okay, Adam One: The mother sells her son to a relative. Who lives abroad. She may or may not know the purpose. But she needs the money. For her other children. Then the mother disappears—she's killed. And the boy is delivered to our city. Three days later, the buyer, who is from the boy's country, or nearby, possibly the relative, he closes in. He poisons the boy with a traditional potion, the beans, paralyzes him. Then he cuts the boy's throat, while the boy is still alive, drains the blood, cuts off the head, the hands, the feet, dumps the remaining corpse into moving water. All this to give the man a power boost—more money, more followers, maybe to prevail in a legal dispute, maybe with a landlord, like they said."

"And," I interjected, "this man, he leaves the head, hands, and feet just lying around in the building. What? For later? And he takes the ceremonial bottle to a pawnshop for a little cash?"

"Right."

"Anyway, this would be the dark guy in the video," I said.

My wife continued: "Or, a variation: It wasn't the dark guy in the video who did it, but some other person, but yes, a witch doctor, and that witch doctor left behind the head, the hands, the feet, and the bottle, and the junkie later came upon the crime scene and scavenged the bottle and took it down to the pawnshop to support his habit, but the junkie otherwise had nothing to do with it. So still Adam One, black-magic murder, Adam One-A."

"Possibly," I agreed.

"Or Adam Two," she began. "Because I don't believe Adam One or One-A."

"Me, neither."

"Adam Two: Adam fled the country. He escaped. His mother didn't sell him."

"Fled the country. By himself?"

"Well, yes. Maybe. Maybe somebody there put him on a plane. Best they could do."

"But then he didn't. Didn't get away," I said.

"No."

"He was killed nonetheless," I said.

"Yes. But, Adam Two, it could have been the white guy in the video who did the deed," my wife said.

"Mm."

"But who is he to kill a seven-year-old boy? A refugee? And cut off his head?" she asked. "Just to get the bottle? Was there something else to steal?"

"Either way, the boy tried to escape his fate, and couldn't," I said.

"Mm. But look: Why would the three to five *days* or three to five *months* matter to the philosopher?" she said, circling back. "In our city. The time frame."

"Uh-huh . . ."

"Well, suppose their reasoning is this: If the boy had been *here* only three to five days, then he could have been *there*, in his country, around the time those people were buried. The new grave, the grave of forty plus three."

"And since it appears that his mother is in that grave—"

"Oh, she is."

"So he could have been there or nearby. We've got this boy in his country at the probable *time* of his mother's death. And so was he also at the *place*?"

"Right. He'd be one of the three who got away."

"Right."

We paused.

My wife continued: "But anyway, if he had been here only three to five *days*—which he had—and if somebody curious started to probe where he was before he left, why he left, they could stumble upon it; they could discover that incident, those forty people killed. Maybe more elsewhere. The boy's case would lead them to our other case."

"They don't know that we already know."

"Right. And it may not be us they're most worried about," she said. "But on the other hand, if he'd been here three to five *months*, as they wish, questions about where he came from would miss the critical time period."

"And meanwhile here—"

"If they can say it was a black-magic sacrifice—"

"End of story," I said.

"Exactly."

We paused again.

"So are there more graves—recent? That people there could show us?" she asked.

An airplane, on its way to land, glided overhead, the plane in the last sunlight, the city below in early dark. Then the plane disappeared toward the airport, invisible below our horizon of buildings and trees. We watched the clouds; my wife sat up.

"Evidence, thinking. That should be us. Our plan. But events are passing us by."

The cat moved onto her lap and looked at me with his green eyes like he was looking at rain out through window glass.

"Maybe there's something we missed in that pawnshop video," my wife said.

"Maybe."

"Or maybe . . . Remember the junior officer?" she asked.

"Middle drawer."

"Right."

"Do we trust him? How did the page of doodles get passed on?" I said.

"We don't know. But we don't have a lot of options. He seemed possibly willing . . ."

"Right. Okay."

We went downstairs, the cat following, and instead of sleep, we prepared, into the night, a lengthy update and set of questions, which we sent to the junior officer in Township C.

LOOK

We'd had a rough evening at the other lab, an evening on to past midnight, as we finally could no longer avoid assembling and collating the photographic evidence from our off-record excavations, the nongovernmental digs at the old graves on the terraces, and the recent one, the grave of forty plus three. Picture after picture, for hours: the bones, how they were arrayed, indicating how the person died, the struggle, or none; the angle of the skull indicating the direction of the last look; the stature, the hip width, indicating man or woman; deformities indicating not enough to eat; nicks or marks or healed breaks indicating accidents survived, violence endured; the eyes, the mouth, the ears, holes through which desire had entered, the brain shell now empty of what it once wanted; proximity to other bones indicating who died together or were transported together; remaining clothing indicating a belief in a hidden self, in dignity; any watches not stolen indicating a belief in time; books or letters or diaries indicating a belief in civilization, a belief in others; remaining rope binding arms and legs, blindfolds over eyes, indicating the executioners' fear of the living; numbers and numbers and numbers of bones indicating insanity unleashed. All that and more, surmised, imagined, deducted from the uncovered bones and materials, mostly just bones, the nothing that was the person now released into serene air.

All of it usable someday as evidence. But no way to wash our brains back to shiny and bright.

When the last photo had been put into some kind of analytical order, we left that lab. It was the middle of the night. We went to the park, to the dangerous part of it. We had not been sleeping much; we had not been sleeping well. My wife told me that the reason we were together was that she wanted to disappear into me; she wanted to become me, not herself. Alternately, I would be the window she would jump out of. I told her I wasn't happy to have her hooked on me in that way. I didn't want that kind of guarantee. We needed some other kind of fix if we were going to have a future after this investigation, these investigations.

When we got home, we slid the chest of drawers over in front of our bedroom door to block entry. We lay on the floor with our lab clothes still on, and simply fell asleep. But not for long. We joined the insomniacs down by the river. The sun rose. We spent most of the day there, by the water, under the trees. It seemed that the disturbed could detect something even more disturbing about us. They kept their distance. Midday, we went up into town to a deli. My wife stated her order; the man at the counter looked up at her and stopped. I repeated her order to him. He got to work. Lunch. Back to the river. My wife wanted to swim. I convinced her the water was

132   *Not Long Ago Persons Found*

too polluted. Also I was concerned, though I didn't say it, that she would dive under and never come back up. End of day, night falling, we headed to our legitimate lab, at headquarters. At the loading dock door, my wife went in; I went down the street to get a take-out dinner. When I arrived at the lab later, Room A was dark, a projector on a counter spilling a part of the pawnshop video onto a blank space on the wall. She had the video slowed down and zoomed tight, the images blown into shards of pixels, sharp edges of colors, blacks and whites jerking, popping, colliding, like traffic accidents, like elemental chaos, prior to life. The sound, slowed too, disaggregated the footfalls of the two men down into primal jolts, deep rock faults slipping, releasing the voice of a large animal, the first. My wife was wrecked and sobbing at the projector. She was in the cold again, talking to herself. She wouldn't let me touch her. She said she couldn't make sense of it. Somewhere in there was Adam's killer. I set down our dinner. The door between our two functions, our two inquiries, was broken.

We heard a noise behind us. My wife swung the projector around. It caught a human figure, hand forward in front of its eyes, being stabbed by light from the video. It was the philosopher. He went to the wall, waved his hands. I'd broken the motion detector a few days before. He found the override switch. The room flooded with broad, color-balanced, energy-efficient illumination. The philosopher looked at us, my wife a ruin and me in full inaction.

"Where were you two?" he asked.

We didn't answer. He shook his head and left the room, the air-lock door sucking closed behind him.

"What if I just have to leave?" my wife said to me in the aftermath.

"And go where?"

"You'd hear from me."

"I'm staying?" I asked.

"You have to."

I objected, but she was right. Our house was always in some kind of state. Rain could come through the roof anytime, sluicing into the living room. And if that happened, I had to be there for it.

Two days later we got a message back from the junior officer. He wrote:

> The luggage shop owners confirmed to me that they'd sold a suitcase, similar to the one in the picture you attached, to a woman they believe to be the mother of the boy in your other picture. They admitted also to their belief that the boy's mother and possibly the boy's father, and possibly other relatives, have disappeared. If they know more, they won't say, not under normal questioning.
>
> And for your queries to the gift shop clerk, first as to the potion: I showed him the list of ingredients that were said to be in the medicine that was fed to the boy before the killing, the beans and the rest. The clerk confirmed that the beans are a

traditional agent used to keep a victim immobile but alive for an initial bloodletting. But the gold flakes, clay pellets, and other items on the list, that mix seemed confused, at cross-purposes, not thought through.

A propos, the clerk reported that right after the time of the disappearances in our area, a northerner had been at the gift shop, asking a lot of questions. The clerk refused to sell him any beans, as he thought the man was not competent to use them. Though of course it is possible for anybody to buy beans like that in various shops or markets.

Second, as to the head, hands, and feet: The clerk said that abandoning these in an empty building was wasteful, suggesting haste or negligence, or ignorance. The clerk said that a practitioner in their tradition who would sacrifice a human could be deviant, could be evil, but would not be sloppy with the body parts.

Third, who could have killed the boy or ordered it, could it have been the boy's uncle: The clerk said again that whoever did this killing was incompetent or in an unholy hurry. He said again that the sacrifice of a human is not common in their medicine. It is considered to be selfish and disruptive, a violation, unbalancing. If done despite that, it would not be done by a close relative; it would have to be different clans. The uncle would never be involved in any way, for fear that the whole thing would turn back on him.

And finally, the victim's body in the river: The clerk said that releasing the remains into moving water—your river—was as prescribed. I told him that where the body was released, it would have required many tides for it to float out to open water, the sea, which it did not do. I asked the clerk if it would have been appropriate to weight the body to sink, so it wouldn't be found and removed from the water by others, and the body used by them for their purposes. He said the question was too disturbing; he couldn't answer it. He said a true practitioner, even one on the dark side, would know how to respect the remains of the sacrifice, to allow the boy's spirit to be freed. He said that the cruelty to this young man and the disrespect for his body had been meant to send a message, and the message had been received.

Then the clerk terminated the interview and left the police station.

My dear colleagues, people here know who the boy is who died in your city. They knew who he was without your forensics. And what happened to him has added to their terror. It has been demonstrated, by this example, that if they defy their government, if they try to escape, they will be tracked down, anywhere, and the manner of their termination will be the worst they can imagine.

The next day I sought out the clerk again—I won't say where—for a second interview. He was not cooperative. He said only that in the evening, down by the river, he'd seen a doctor in a black cap and black surgical gown riding a white horse upstream at full gallop, the doctor raking the horse's side with a sharp spur, leaving gashes. I asked the clerk, if he saw them again, to get a close look at the doctor's face, so that maybe we could identify him. The clerk sent me a message the day after that. He said that the horse is terrified and won't let him near.

 The clerk said also that he'd heard some things related to himself. Subsequently, he has become difficult to find.

We sent a copy of the junior officer's message over to the server at the other lab with a disguised subject heading, and we deleted, we hoped, any trace of it in our headquarters accounts. Electronic smuggling. We were beginning to prepare for the worst.

And as to the beans, it was about time. We went to the university, to the department of botany. We were directed to the office where we had been a few days before to deliver the samples of the supposed potion from the boy's stomach, the samples that we'd stolen that one night from the lab at headquarters. Now, upon our return, the office door was open; the professor was in a chair behind his desk, his back to us, looking out the window. We entered. My wife recited the Latin name—genus and species—of the trees he was looking at.

"Not native," she added.

"Mm," the professor said, not turning around.

"Did you have a look at the material?" she asked.

"The report is on the desk," he said.

And there, on his otherwise bare desk, was a printout of a few pages on university letterhead, the text turned to face us.

"How long has this been ready?" my wife asked.

"Awhile."

"Were you going to let us know?"

"Yes."

She picked up the report. He swung around in his chair to face us. He looked like he was about to leave to go fishing.

"That's the report I'm supposed to give you," he said.

"Oh?"

"It says it was a mix, a traditional potion, of the paralytic beans plus flakes of gold and quartz, clay pellets, rare earths, bone splinters, and chopped roots of sacred plants. The additives considered as offerings to spiritual powers."

My wife and the botanist looked at each other across the desk for some time.

"So that's bogus," she said.

"Indeed it is," he replied.

"Somebody got to you."

"I'm a realist."

"Who was it?"

"I have many former students, besides yourself, out there in the world, trying to earn a living in their own way."

"Who? How did they know you had this sample?"

"You could have been a serious botanist, if you had chosen to."

"I've disappointed you."

"Actually, the opposite. But I do what I must. Almost."

He reached into his bottom desk drawer, pulled out a different set of printouts, on plain paper, placed this on the desk.

"This is the real report," he said. "Please keep it confidential."

My wife dropped the official report back onto the desk, next to the plain report, left them both lying there.

"Where the two reports agree is on the beans," the botanist said, then stopped.

"We're listening," I said.

"Those beans likely having the effects as advertised: partial paralysis of a subject to be sacrificed in advance of the actual . . ."

"Yes."

"And a footnote: the paralytic agent, the beans. The intent, with a correct dose, is that the victim's vocal apparatus is not affected."

He paused to observe the beginning of her reaction. Then he continued.

"The victim would be able to scream while being cut. Because it is believed that the screams give additional power to the sacrifice, and the body parts and blood harvested."

"Oh," my wife said, slumping. The botanist invited us to sit down, and we did.

"And where are the beans from? Your assessment?"
I asked.

"Based on mineral content, some insect residue, and phenotype, I'd say the beans were from the boy's country of origin. That general area."

"Okay," my wife said. "And the rest, the other ingredients? Really?"

The botanist put his finger on the plain report.

"Bits of aluminum foil, bits of plastic, bits of chopped-up lettuce, tomatoes, pickles, and potatoes, bits of salt and pepper, splinters from wood toothpicks, and a substrate of tomato-based and mustard seed–based pastes. You see what I'm saying?"

"Yes."

"I suppose nonetheless it could have been a local practitioner, who knew how to use the beans but was fuzzy about the rest, or had to improvise," the botanist said.

"Do you know of any local practitioners?" my wife asked.

"No. No. Nobody who would participate in this."

We were all quiet for a moment.

"Okay, we'll go," I said.

"It's depressing, isn't it," the professor said, "what was done to that boy, what's happening to you."

"What's happening to us?" I asked.

"Oh. You'll need to find that out for yourselves," he said.

"Why don't you join our group?" my wife asked. "Help us?"

"Which group?"

"Don't pretend," she said.

"Well okay, yes. But I'm not on a side."

"Seems to me you are."

Nothing. We got up, went to his door, looked back. We left both reports on his desk.

"I'll think about it," he said. We all paused a moment; then I asked, "You going fishing?"

"Probably," he said.

"Why don't you get on with it, then?"

"In due time."

He swiveled his chair around again to look out the window into the trees.

We left the botanist's office at the university and made our way over to our unsafe park, to the path of plunder, the corridor of opportunity, the place where we could think properly and privately. At a dark point on the path, between lights, my wife stopped us.

"What *is* happening to us?" she asked me.

"One thing is we're losing this job, our project," I said. "It's falling apart."

"What kind of career is this? What am I doing? Where are we going to end up?" she asked.

"Look at that guy, your old prof."

"Maybe he could come around."

"I doubt it," I said.

I turned, continued walking. She followed, two steps behind, worrying on, talking to my back.

"We've been in this boy's bones, in his lungs, his

stomach; we've looked inside his brain. All this investigation and we still haven't got ahold of motivation. Why did he come here? How much had he seen? Did he have an aspiration, hope for something, anything? At seven, you'd expect he'd possess an almost indestructible will to live. Did he still have that?"

I didn't reply.

"And now the best we can do is send his corpse back home? We've failed him," she said.

I didn't reply.

"Does someone in the headquarters building have a plan for us, you and me?" she asked.

I didn't reply.

"Is this going to trash us, too? Am I losing you?" she asked.

I didn't reply. I didn't reply, and I didn't turn around to face you, which now, years later, I regret. But at that moment, I had nothing for you.

By then, it was late, as always. We'd meet with the philosopher the next morning, on little sleep, as always. When we got home, the cat was right inside the door. I thought he might reconsider, but he went straight to my wife again, avoiding me. She picked him up and wandered off, whispering to him, telling him things she would never tell me.

TAKE

This meeting with the philosopher was the first since he'd found us, after hours, lost in the pawnshop video. My wife started in before we even sat down.

"What if it wasn't black magic? she said. "The evidence is suspicious. Maybe it was a fake."

The philosopher looked impatient. My wife forged ahead.

"The bottle from the pawnshop was carrying river water, not any kind of potion. It probably belonged to the boy. Probably water from his river. Why, we don't know. A talisman, for protection, for luck, maybe a gift."

"Didn't bring him much luck, did it? Okay, it was a gift. For the male relative."

"If there is such a person in our city. But even if there is a relative, and if it was witchcraft, it never would have been that relative, or any relative, who killed the boy. Not within the family, not within the clan. Even in black magic there are rules."

"You know there's a reporter on this now," the philosopher said.

"We don't know," she replied. "And the so-called potion in the boy's stomach . . ."

"A local TV reporter," the philosopher continued, nodding up to his murmuring screen.

"We haven't had much time for TV."

"You're missing something. She has an influence. She's giving the story a shape. You know, the human, a human shape. In any case, yes, the *potion*, it did have poison beans in it? To paralyze the boy? Up to the moment he was cut and bled? Let him scream? The horror? Right?"

"Yes, there were poisonous beans. But the rest . . ."

"Gold flakes, bone splinters, rare earths, pellets of clay, chopped roots of sacred plants—a *potion*, offerings to the dark spirits. Right?"

"What was in the so-called potion were bits of aluminum foil, traces of salt and pepper, splinters from wood toothpicks, chopped-up lettuce, tomatoes, pickles, and french fries, and traces of catsup and mustard. Sir, the boy had had nothing to eat for a day and he was fed the remains of somebody's fast-food dinner. Together with the beans, to make them go down, and to make it look spooky."

"Who told you that?" the philosopher asked.

"Who told you otherwise?" my wife said.

"Seriously now, who did your work on the beans?" the philosopher insisted. "It wasn't in our lab."

"Says who?" my wife asked.

Here the philosopher realized he was close to revealing that he had a spy in the lab we were using at headquarters. He hummed for a moment, then dodged.

"Well, okay, I suppose so. Those other materials. Fast food. Okay. So some witch doctor who has immigrated here, probably illegally, he got the authentic beans but had to improvise the rest. Maybe having a fuzzy memory, he finessed the potion. Still, the intent. Black magic, a human sacrifice."

"There's more," my wife said. "The head and hands. Use of the cut-off body parts would be one of the primary benefits of a sacrifice. If it had been a black-magic priest, killing a human, he would have taken it seriously; he would have been careful with every product of the butchering. In this case, the head and feet down by a furnace that hadn't functioned for two years, the hands up on the roof in a hamburger bag—these are the products of a disorganized mind. If this was a witch doctor, he was incompetent or not thinking straight."

"I've heard that before. Do you have anything else?" the philosopher asked.

"Not thinking straight except for this: The body dumped in the river, not weighted to sink, where it would take three tides to float to open water—the body was meant to be found."

"Okay, meant to be found. A curse, like when they stick pins into a doll's head. And as for the parts, the head, et cetera, they went for the blood instead. The body was drained of blood. It's still black magic, whatever their purposes. Their dark purposes."

"The blood could have been drained by time in the water," my wife said. "Sir, the black-magic angle seems botched, a cover-up, or a sideshow, badly executed."

"What about the people there who sold the suitcase to the boy's mother? What do they know?" I added.

"Why don't you go ask them?" the philosopher countered. "On your dime. Distractions, distractions. Who is your expert, your cultural consultant? About the ceremony, the uncle, the use of the parts?"

"Mm," my wife said. We knew the gift shop clerk had gone into hiding. "A colleague at the university."

"Yeah, I don't think so," the philosopher said. "Your expert is not going to appear, is he? Basically, what do you have? Nothing. And we have something, which is this, this TV reporter now: The boy flees his country, but death pursues him. His destiny is stalking him, in the form of a dark priest, from his place of birth, a violent country. The priest bought the boy, bought the rights to the boy. For the belief, the superstition, that the sacrifice of a young human, and the blood, forget the body parts, would be a source of power. For the priest or a client. Power the person did not feel living here. The long, dark tentacles reach up from the boy's primitive countryside into our city, and *rauwp*! they take the boy. It was his fate."

My wife stood up, pointed a finger at the philosopher. If it had been a gun, it would have been aimed at his brain.

"This wasn't fate; it was a crime," she said to our boss. "And when we know enough, we will nail the killer."

"When will you know enough?"

"We're not action heroes."

"Yeah, I noticed that."

"It takes time."

"Right. On your own, then," the philosopher said. He was looking at my wife's finger, still pointed at his head. I knew the feeling. She'd done this before, aimed at me.

The philosopher pushed the finger, and her hand, and her arm, to the side. She remained standing.

"This is moving fast," he continued, "and at this juncture we just need you to get out of the way. So, how do you know the general?"

The philosopher looked at us both with a small smile, then went on.

"You told our contractor down there that you know the general, that he was your supervisor."

"We don't. Know him," I said.

"Supervisor for what? I'm your supervisor."

"It was expeditious to use his name at the time. A tight situation."

"I see. A little subterfuge. You two."

My wife sat down.

What we had done was to claim to the fixer at the airport that the general was in charge of our other project, the off-record digs, and now this misinformation had arrived back here as mis-misinformation. Better for us, I supposed.

The philosopher took a sip from a glass of clear liquid on his desk. My wife and I figured out, at the same moment, that it wasn't water.

"You're an attractive woman," the philosopher said, leaning back, conveying that he was in an expansive mood that he would share with us. "You must have had other options. How did you get into this? Forensic anthropology. How bizarre. You're not even the medical examiner."

"That's correct."

"The crime scene, the fresh gore."

"Not me."

"What you do, it's the deadest of the dead. Way after they're dead."

"When you know the ending, you have a chance to understand the meaning."

"The meaning. The meaning."

He waved his hands in front of him, as if around something spherical and vague.

"What's the meaning here?" he said. "The boy was a victim, pure and simple. Somebody used him. He did nothing. He's snuffed; he's dead. Eradicated. A data blip. Where's the meaning in that?"

"We give him back his meaning by figuring out who killed him. Who and why," my wife said.

"Is that so?"

"We use the evidence. We use our brains. We tell the boy, 'We know who killed you and that person will be stopped.' Otherwise, we're just crying and moaning."

"We tell the boy nothing. Because he's dead. Unless you talk to the dead."

"We do."

"That's psychotic. Look, nobody has showed up who cares about this child, this corpse. And nobody will. No family—they're all gone."

"You're sure of that."

"I am. We are."

"Then we're his family."

"You're dreaming. You expect a resolution because you are privileged. You expect neatness and order."

"We try."

"Well, give it up. Where this boy's from, he's just another dead body. They don't have time."

"Have you asked them?"

"Oh, you're tiring. Let's get practical. At this point, what is *our* interest? What is it that *we* need? We've got this reporter. There's a story floating, so to speak. We need to tell the public that the murderer has been identified, so they can go back to their little lives. And the black-magic angle, so much the better. Ooh, the head and hands were cut off. It's our police against the forces of evil out there, the heathen, the primitives, the rest of the world."

"And then what?" he continued. "We're down to a bureaucratic hassle between our immigration control and their consulate. All anybody needs is a story, as I've said, and we've got one."

He indicated a form on his computer screen.

"See here, this box, this page. We fill in how he was killed, the likely who; we complete the page, a copy to them, the form in the file to our server, a paper copy in a drawer, a scan to doc storage. So copies everywhere no one will look at, and we're done." He clapped his hands off each other like slapping off dirt.

"And the body?" my wife asked.

"The reassembled parts. Yes. Someone in their consulate, in that busy staff person's spare time, will work on getting the body repatriated."

"Probably never."

"That's right. More forms. Lots of forms . . ."

The philosopher emptied his glass, then looked longingly over at his minibar against the wall section that was also his secret back door. It was going to be time for us to leave soon. He turned back, looked at my wife, looked at me, took another detour.

"You're not technically married, you two."

My wife laughed; I did not. Then she replied, "So what?" to the philosopher, and looked to me. I hesitated but said that what she and I had was as good as . . . was the same as . . .

"Or not," the philosopher interjected. "In a legal proceeding, one of you could testify against the other."

My wife looked to me again. I held her gaze. I confess that at that moment, I wanted you to feel it: that I possibly could, that you possibly could. I wanted you to feel why not.

After this delay, I turned back to the philosopher and said, "If you could make one of us do that. Testify."

"Uh-huh," the philosopher grunted, considering us both. Then quietly but clearly, he said, "We could." He paused.

"Could you," my wife replied, just as quiet, just as clear.

Another stare-down between them.

Then the philosopher said to her, "Well, I get it. You work with dead people because you're too obstinate for the rest of us."

She said nothing.

"So you see, there is some discontent from above with your fit in this organization, with your consideration of the needs of the team, the commitments you agreed to when you were hired. What you signed. So now your work is done and we are reducing your security clearance again—to gray. Effective immediately. You'll need to get permission to get into your lab, or anywhere else in the building."

He was looking at my wife. We were careful not to look at each other. I believe we shared a thought: that the philosopher was not aware that I had security codes, too.

"Opossum, opossum, ohh—pohhhhh—sssssummm," the philosopher said.

The wall section with his minibar on it rotated a quarter turn. A view of the landing outside and the sound of the deep, empty stairwell called to us. We got up, went out, and had started down the first step when we heard the philosopher yell "Newt newt newt," and the secret door lurched, skreaked, and closed behind us. The department name stenciled on the outside of his door had been painted over and changed again. Now it was the BUREAU OF PERPETUAL EXPLANATION. The lettering was still wet.

"Did you notice any paint on the philosopher's hands?" my wife whispered.

"No," I whispered back. "He has no fucking . . ."

"Get going," we heard a tiny philosopher say, his voice coming from a tiny camera-mike-speaker device above his door.

I started to make a gesture. My wife caught my hand as if her love runneth over; then she spun us both around such that our backs were to the philosopher's electronic eye.

"Then who?" she whispered, continuing her train of thought. About the name repainting.

"A joker loose in the building," I whispered.

She agreed. She continued to restrain my one arm, which she held. I could have used my other arm, but I didn't. We began to ka-plunk our way on down the reverberating stairs.

Two levels lower, I stopped us, pointed to the door there, to the department names painted on it. One of the functions on that floor was evidence storage. I signaled to my wife to be quiet and for her to try the door lock. Her code already didn't work. I tried mine. The door opened.

We went down a corridor to a heavy door labeled EVIDENCE. My code worked again. We entered. Rows and rows of shelves and bins in there, on them and in them the objects, fluids, and documents being held as witnesses in cases still open. It was like an auto junkyard, each defunct vehicle or part with a history, and somewhere still to go. All this salvage was for murders and thefts and negligence and aggressions not yet resolved, somebody alive still hoping for a reason why, an assignment of guilt. For one case, just a set of false teeth, upper and lower, the only speakers for whatever had happened there. Evidence for solved cases was moved to a warehouse closer to the river.

We found the high, wide shelf for Adam. On it were his suitcase and two boxes, one box containing the clay bottle with two birds on it, the original of the video from the pawnshop, and some handwritten notes. In the other box were the shorts that the corpse had been wearing when it was found, Adam's new city library card, and a collection of small belongings and materials that had been taken from the room he'd been sleeping in, the nights after his arrival and before his murder.

One thing we did not find was the red cord with yellow stripes that the gift shop clerk had told us to look for because Adam could have been wearing it around his neck.

We pulled out the notes that were in the box with the pawnshop video. These were the comments that the police detectives had written during their reviews and handoffs and rereviews of the video. The dark man in the pawnshop was nobody that anybody knew; they would look for him. The white man was a known junkie who frequented that part of downtown, and even the very building, where Adam's head and other missing parts were found. The junkie, in one opinion, could have come upon the scene after the sacrifice and taken the bottle for drug money. In another opinion, the junkie was also a sometime errand boy for law enforcement. The penultimate note was a single line: "The junkie works for the agency." And below that, in a different hand: "No touchy." The notes ended there.

We put the clay bottle, the original of the pawnshop video, and the library card into Adam's suitcase. We thought we heard a noise to our left, and there, at the end of that row of shelves, we might have glimpsed a small body, draped in an autopsy sheet, with red lines at its neck, wrists, and ankles. It could have been observing us. Now it was disappearing around the corner.

We rolled the suitcase with the evidence down to the

end of that shelf row. Down past the ends of all the shelf rows was the evidence vault exit door, gliding shut, as though someone had just gone through it. We towed the suitcase out that door to the corridor, and out the final door onto the landing in the silo of exit stairs. We stopped and smiled at each other, the stolen suitcase with its stolen goods by our side. I think this was the moment I most wish we could return to, that I could return to.

From the landing outside the evidence room, I picked up the suitcase and carried it as we drummed our way down to street level. There, I beckoned to my wife and we continued two more levels down, through that entry door, down a corridor, and through another door into the cold room. We rolled the suitcase in as if arriving in a rebel camp.

Filling the perimeter walls, on three sides, were banks of drawer fronts, stacked from floor to neck height and side by side, as if for cabinets of paper files, but these drawer fronts were double-sized, with a hard hand latch at the top, and behind the fronts were chilled corpses on slide-out shelves. These were the bodies, or just parts, for open cases, or remains not yet claimed by family. Offenses against them still alive in them, most of these corpses had objects related to them stored in the active evidence room upstairs. This body vault was new but filling up fast.

A few of the drawer fronts were opened, tipped down, the shelves inside pushed partway out, and on these shelves, against these shelves, sitting, standing, leaning, were ghosts of the deceased, the newly dead, not straying far from their bodies, not yet.

The cold room, in a touch of beautiful insanity, also had its own TV monitors, two flat screens angled down from ceiling brackets, facing each other, tuned to different channels, like in a sports bar, their conflicting audios turned down low. Some of the spirits on the shelves were looking at the monitors, some not, some looking at one another, as if trying to figure out how to talk, what language to use, or what to say next. Two of them had a game of 3-D chess going, stacking up on an empty shelf suspended between them. The hours in the body vault were long, their future uncertain; none of them slept. It was like a prison common room, the physical corpses wrapped in orange zip bags, in case any might try to escape.

I scanned the room, found the phantom that had been pursuing us. He was out, seated on his shelf, young legs dangling, looking around, trying to figure out how to be in his new world. Adam. Did he know us? Did he see us? Hard to tell.

If I'd wanted these beings to be our allies, I ought to have behaved differently, but what I did was grab the handle of an autopsy gurney, yank it over, unzip the evidence suitcase, extricate the two-birds clay bottle, and slam the bottle down on the metal gurney top in front of Adam. He flinched and shuddered. His dangling legs stopped swinging. My wife touched my arm.

"Also ineffective," I said to her, pointing to the bottle. "River water. It didn't protect him. He's dead."

"You're dead," I said to Adam. He looked around him

again. My wife sighed but waited there with me as I stared at essentially nothing.

What did he do then, the young man? What could he do? He faded, disaggregated, disappeared. They all did. Each one, one at a time, looked our way, shook his or her head no, then vanished, the cold room gone empty, the body drawers closed, fronts up, the two TVs whispering the news. My wife told me it was okay, we had to let them leave this world eventually, what it did to them, let them leave it to us.

I thought the clay bottle should remain there, empty, on the gurney. But my wife returned the bottle to the suitcase, zipped the suitcase up, put its handle in my hand, rolled the gurney back to its place with the others.

"We should go," she said. "We're not welcome here."

We left.

All this we saw and did, and, as with so much, we never talked about it again.

We rolled the suitcase—the bottle, the pawnshop video, the library card, and the rest inside—out to the stair landing for subbasement 2. I carried the suitcase up to street level, where we turned left toward the loading dock. There we set off an alarm. Probably the suitcase had been chipped and we'd just crossed a sensor.

The alarm speakers started a sequence of whoops and bleats, some of them broken by defects in the audio system—a cracked speaker, a loose wire, a corrupted sound file. The huge roll door started to descend. When we got to the side man door, it had already locked itself. My wife grabbed the suitcase handle from me, ran with the case behind her, and dove under the rolling door just before it slammed down. She and the suitcase were on the dock outside. I was locked inside.

I returned to the house after midnight, after the interrogations.

"What did you say?" she asked me.

"Don't worry, I protected you," I said.

Which turned out to be not totally difficult. Security for the building had been hired out, and they better have been cheap, at least, because the guards confronting me were a combination of decrepit and inept. They did cuff my arms and legs into difficult positions for some intervals while they continued their belligerent and illogical questions. It was as if they'd got their procedural manual from watching television. As such, it could have taken a turn for the worse, but fortunately in my case, it did not.

"Weren't you happy that one of us got out? With the evidence?" my wife asked.

Yes, I was.

She said that she'd been trying to get a lawyer to me.

On the kitchen table, she'd set out a bottle of bourbon, some ice, and two glasses. I went to the table, picked up the empty glasses, carried them to the sink, and threw them in. They shattered. My wife and I, the scientist and the translator, we called this "speaking through objects."

It took an hour to remove all the broken glass from the sink, the counter, and the floor. An hour less sleep.

That night, the cat made a decision. After his days of observation, of scrutinizing, after the broken glass had been cleaned up, he jumped up on the kitchen counter, stared at me. We touched noses; he looked into my eyes, stopped purring, jumped down. Then he wouldn't let me touch him at all, no way, wouldn't let me anywhere near him. I tried to corner him, but he was too quick. I never would have hurt the cat in any way, but something was going on with me that he didn't want to be around. I told him I was a good man in a bad place temporarily. That changed nothing.

The next morning we dispatched a copy of the pawnshop video on a flash drive, plus the clay bottle, to the junior officer by special courier. We put the original of the video and Adam's library card into the suitcase, and the suitcase went downstairs to our storage. We couldn't find the cat. Giving up the search, we sat down to talk about our future. There were rumors that the territory to the north was still free. Would she go there first, alone, me to follow, if ever? If we stayed in our city together, what would happen to us? The people upstairs at headquarters, how would they dispose of us? How could we complete our other investigation, the mass graves? Were the people in our other group safe? How much money did we have in the bank?

I thought we might never see the cat again, because of me. But I hoped that for the sake of my wife, he would decide to return.

FATE

To do what, we hadn't a clue, but we went to the lab at headquarters later that same morning, invited by a concerned call from our chief lab tech. Now we had to pass through the lobby receptionist and layers of security. Finally, to expedite, we said we had an appointment with the chief tech, giving her name. She came out to the corridor to greet us. Her white lab smock had two new military-style epaulets on the shoulders: black, with three white stripes each.

"Those are new," my wife said, pointing to the epaulets.

The lab tech smiled. She had been promoted, and the lab coat upgrade invented for her. Did we like the coat, she asked us, smiling wider, the smile that wins at job interviews. She was a prime candidate to have been the rat in the lab, the one who'd been spying on us.

"You're just in time," she said next.

She escorted us into the lab, showed us to our respective desks, which had been cleaned up for us. She pointed to the TV monitors around the space, showing the news. She had patched the news audio into the lab's public-address

160   *Not Long Ago Persons Found*

speakers. She'd always been the most skillful; that's why she was chief tech.

"Wait," she said.

Ten minutes later, on the TV news was a live feed coming from the pressroom downstairs.

The chief of security was at the dais, the lectern loaded with microphones. Behind him were the original detectives for Adam's case, looking disoriented, and the philosopher, putting on his best, most serious mug, but with an inebriated smirk sneaking through.

The chief spoke, through staccato swarms of camera clicks, saying there had been breakthroughs in the case of the immigrant boy whose body had been found floating in our river one year ago. The boy had been given a name by the concerned detectives: Adam. Pollen found in Adam's lungs had been traced to a river valley in a country to the south with a past history of violence and primitive religious practices. Based on investigations in the field and months of scientific analysis, they could now say that Adam had been the victim of a black-magic ritual, whose procedures included the taking of blood and parts of the body even as the boy was still alive.

Murmurs from the press corps, a burst of camera activity.

"Human sacrifice and the blood and body parts harvested in this way are believed, in their religion, to confer special powers to the perpetrator or anybody the parts were sold to."

"A horrific detail," the chief said, then paused for all cameras to be raised, "was that prior to the actual killing, the boy was fed a traditional potion that left him paralyzed but still conscious. The last thing this boy saw, in his young life, was his murderer approaching him with a knife. A fate he could see but not stop. The paralytic that the boy had been fed prevented him from moving his arms or legs, but allowed him to scream, as it is believed that the screams of the victim provide additional potency to the sacrifice and its by-products."

Members of the press corps gasped and muttered, the philosopher looked as dour as he could, the detectives looked dismayed to be a part of this. The chief continued.

"This boy was sold by his mother to a male relative. She should have known the purpose. The boy was transported to our city, where the man who bought him performed the bloodletting and dismemberment. These people are their own worst enemies," he said, looking up gravely from his prepared text.

"The mother has not been located, but is being pursued in the boy's country of origin. A female relative of the mother, who may have served as an intermediary and who may have kept the boy with her for some time while he was in transit, is living in a city near us, and we are seeking to have her extradited. The male relative, the perpetrator, has been living among us as an undocumented alien. He has fled, disappeared, and we are looking for him. We believe it is the man in this picture."

On a screen to the chief's side was projected a frame from the pawnshop video, a moment when the dark man with the exotic hat and shoulder bag was approximately facing the camera. A man that neither we nor the police knew anything about.

Upstairs, the chief lab tech, now lab chief, smiled at us again.

My wife said, "That man has no link to Adam that we know of, no link to Adam's family that we know of, no link even to Adam's country."

"He'll do," the lab chief said. "He looks the part."

She stood over us. We were seated at our cleared desks. "What shall we do today?" she asked. "Your plan?"

We left. We went to the park. We sent messages to the members of the group around our other investigation. Our trouble could become their trouble. Through the remainder of that day and night, there were no responses except from the director of our other lab, who said that they were going to have to restrict themselves to their official business until something changed, and until then, could we please stay away. We thought to warn the botanist, though we suspected he would take care of himself.

Overnight, at home, we heard back from the junior officer, who wrote:

> Nobody here recognizes the dark man in the pawnshop video that you sent. Not I, not the church gift shop clerk, not the travel shop owners, not other policemen, nobody. That man's clothes, his face, he doesn't look like anybody who'd be from these parts.

The gift shop clerk identified your clay bottle but refused to take it back. Since this contact with him regarding the bottle and the video, the clerk has thoroughly disappeared again. We are supposed to arrest him.

I dropped the bottle into the river near town. Also, that copy of the video. They both sank. I cannot make use of these things here. I'm getting married next month. I have hope for our future.

I will say that while I didn't recognize the dark man in the pawnshop, I did recognize the white man. He was one of the trainers for an intensive I took in your city.

End of message. And while we were absorbing that, a second message arrived, consisting only of these numbers: 35:17:12. It took a while to guess that this message had come from the gift shop clerk, at some cost, given his present circumstances, and that the numbers might be referring to the pawnshop video. We cued up the video to the nominal thirty-fifth minute, seventeenth second, twelfth frame. And there was a clear view of the white man, facing the camera full front, on his way out of the pawnshop, after the sixty seconds in which the clay bottle had been exchanged for cash. In this frame, zoomed down, looking closely, we could make out a red cord with three yellow stripes around the white man's neck.

We cross-checked with the single front image of Adam from the airport cameras on the day that he arrived. Zooming in: a red cord with yellow stripes visible around

Adam's neck. The cord that the gift shop clerk told us to look for, the cord that was supposed to keep Adam from harm.

"The junkie in the pawnshop, he killed Adam," my wife said. "Took the bottle, took the red cord, sold the bottle, put the cord around his own neck. I hope the cord serves him well."

The white man, the drug addict, a part-time contractor for the agency, a part-time trainer for foreign cops, had been given the assignment to track down Adam and eliminate him. Why? Because of what Adam had seen: the murder of his mother and the others in the grave of forty plus three. And the rest, the *ritual sacrifice*, the disposition of the body parts? A diversion, a product of the junkie imagination—the enhanced, black ops, half-competent junkie imagination.

Then the philosopher sent us a message, in the form of a marshal, who knocked on our door, rousted us from an almost sleep, and presented us with a summons to be at headquarters by 3:45 that afternoon. We were punctual. The philosopher sat us down, pointed to his TV monitor, where, from the downstairs pressroom, a next step in the Adam drama was unfolding: expert analysis.

In split screens on the monitor were two men, each of whom had written a book. The left-screen man spoke of a once promising culture, now ravaged by superstition, corruption, and violence, people turned against one another.

"Us," my wife interjected.

The philosopher scowled. He picked up a crib sheet of voice codes, scowled again, dropped the crib sheet back on his desk, picked up his manual remote, raised the volume on the TV with that.

The right-screen man spoke of regressive forces still at work in the villages in the boy's native river valley, beliefs and practices of black magic that had not yet been eradicated; how the boy had tried to escape, how the primitive beliefs had pursued him, had reached all the way up to our city, had caught the boy and killed him. "These people are their own worst enemies," he intoned, as grim as grim can be.

Left-screen provided more details about the history and geography of black magic.

As the experts spoke, the philosopher tapped his finger on parts of the press release he had issued, three pages laid out on his desk. He held pages up, showed us phrases from his work being repeated, nearly word for word, by the heads on TV. We'd never seen the philosopher look so happy.

Finally, the program host said, "But there is a new government there now, in the boy's home country, a progressive government, with a hopeful future, correct?"

"Yes, that's correct," right-screen answered, "and they are being provided with aid and support and military and law-enforcement training."

And then the host said that that was where they'd have to leave it.

The philosopher smiled, doused the TV volume,

stacked the sheets of his press notes together, put them to one side, looked to us.

"Sir, this is a fraud. The science is not there," my wife began.

The philosopher picked up a different sheet of paper from his desk, showed it to us. It was a blank sheet, but at the top, the logo, name, and address of our other lab.

"I could print anything I want on this sheet," he said. "About the case, about you. We know what you've been up to. Both of you. Now. We've got two people at the airport who are carrying your passports. Remember your passports? You know what? Those two people don't look anything like you, but they're close enough. We could say that they are you, and make you, you two, undocumented, nobody at all. Consider yourselves lucky that you're just fired."

He sat back, took a drink, went on.

"An anthropologist and a translator. I don't know who's going to pay for that kind of thing anymore. Your clearances and permissions are entirely revoked. You'll not come back into this building again. And if you've got any sense, you'll keep your mouths shut about all of this. So. And we know your botanist. He'll keep quiet. He wasn't difficult. And we will track down your black-magic expert down there. We'll get all of you."

I stood up. The philosopher's eyes widened. He pushed back his chair a bit and reached under his desk.

"A gun?" I asked.

"Panic button. Calls security."

"Can't you just say something? Voice command?"

"We're working on it."

I took a step toward him. He reached deeper under his desk, groping for the button.

I stepped back, walked to his minibar, picked up the bottle standing on it, read the label, took off the cap, smelled it.

"Good vodka?" I asked.

"Only the best."

I left the bottle uncapped, set it down, knocked it over. Then I pushed it again. It rolled, fell, broke on the floor. Delinquent whiffs of vodka began to run loose in the room. I stepped back toward the philosopher; he reached under his desk again. Ah me, menacing, but not a menace.

"Opossum," I said, and invited my wife to stand up. The wall section with the minibar against it lurched and started to rotate, crunching on the glass of the broken bottle. We exited to the back stair landing, went three steps down. "Newt newt newt," we heard the philosopher say, and the wall section rotated closed. The title on his door had been painted over and changed again. Now it was MINISTER OF HISTORY.

We drummed our way down the tall, empty stairwell to street level, where we agreed by signs to continue two floors lower, quietly, the stairwell now breathing with us, to the subbasement. Through the door at that level, down a corridor, and through another door was where Adam and the other unclaimed, unidentified, unresolved bodies lay in the cold room, with TV monitors broadcasting the news for them through the dayless, nightless night.

We tried our codes on the door. This time we were both truly locked out. Adam, in there, was never going home now. His body—the bones, the pollen, the dismemberment cuts—would stay on its shelf, prevented from leaving by a skein of permit applications and transport disagreements and personnel changes, until budget cuts would cause the city to move the cold-room bodies into landfill, dikes against the rising ocean, and then high tides will destroy the dikes and the bodies will wash out to sea, and Adam will learn to swim at last.

We heard a noise above. A young guard, at street level, was looking down at us and at his phone screen. In his other hand was a gun, waving sideways as he used his trigger finger to poke at the phone. Then he holstered the phone, straightened out the gun, and with the barrel he gestured for us to climb the stairs. When we reached his level, he gestured with the gun toward the exit door. We exited. The door pulled shut and locked automatically, the guard looking out at us through the tiny security window, then turning away.

We, too, turned away. A crew had been digging in the alley just outside the door, leaving a pile of rubble beside a narrow trench. We looked down into it. High-speed, high-bandwidth cables, multicolored, being added to the branch coming in from the trunk out under the street. A delirium of new data to be fed into the headquarters building.

A detective story is supposed to be about the restoration of order. I picked up a piece of concrete from the pile by the trench and used it to break the exit door window glass. The alarms inside sounded, sick and interrupted. We ran up the alley, wove ourselves into the pedestrians on the sidewalk, and crossed the street at mid-block, as evasions, though I had, no doubt, been caught on the outside camera when I broke the window. So that was stupid, too.

THE INTRUDER, OR WHAT YOU NEED MAY APPEAR TO YOU FIRST AS A THIEF

When we got home, the lock on our front door was stuck. Someone may have tried to open it without a key. I kicked the door in, splitting the wood frame, another thing that would have to be fixed. We crossed through. I jammed the door closed, using some unread mail as a doorstop.

My wife said, "I wish you were going, too."

"You're leaving?"

"I have to."

"What about me?"

"You have to stay here and break things."

"You're not angry? Aren't you angry?"

"I am, but directed at what?"

"But you, what are you going to . . ."

Just then we realized we weren't alone in the house. I went downstairs to the storage room. A young man I'd never seen before was there, stopped near my music collection, not far from Adam's suitcase. Cornered, trying to get to the stairs to leave, he attacked me. I reacted, fought back, injured his arm, probably broke a forearm bone, a thing I had trained for years to know how to do, a thing I'd trained for years never to do from a state of rage, such as I was in, and for what reason.

Outcrazed, the young man stopped, held his arm. I told him to sit down; he did. My wife appeared at the top of the stairs.

"Call the police," I said.

"But . . ."

"Call the police," I insisted.

She left to do that. I was getting my way, wrong upon wrong, from bad to worse.

After some time, siren blurps, then a policeman at the top of the stairs. He came down, breathing heavily. He handcuffed the intruder, plastic cuffs, whole arm to broken arm, behind the perp's back. The intruder howled; the policeman persisted, dragged the young man up the stairs and out the front door.

After they left, I stopped for a moment; then my hand groped an upper shelf for the stem clippers we'd bought for our garden and never used. I didn't have a plan, not even much of a notion. I found the clippers, dropped them into my pocket, went upstairs.

By the time I got to the street, there were two patrol cars stopped at acute angles in front of our building, and three cops: two men, one woman. The patrol car roof lights were exploding, desynchronized, strafing the dark neighborhood, our house, my wife's face on the porch, with blue, red, amber flashes—the lights like mad taggers whose paint won't stick.

172   *Not Long Ago Persons Found*

Their radios cracked out directions for pursuits and captures all over the city.

I went to one car, then the second, peered in at the intruder, handcuffed and in pain in the backseat. The three police were at some distance from the cars, perfectly triangulated, facing away, each of them in a separate conversation on a cell phone. On a night such as that, procedures could be initiated, wheels could be set to turn, that would cause a young man such as the one in their cage to disappear from the world as he'd known it.

One of the officers came striding back toward their cars, grinning, strobed by the colors of emergency. His natural habitat.

"This is what safety looks like," I said to him.

What he said to me: nothing. He went to the car with the intruder in it, opened the front door, checked the mechanism inside that locked the back doors. His phone rang. He closed the door, walked back out to the perimeter to talk.

I peered in to the backseat of the patrol car again. The three police were not paying attention. I opened the front door of the car, found the control, unlocked the back doors, closed the front door, opened one back door, gestured the captive out. I took the garden clippers from my pocket, cut off his handcuffs. His broken arm flopped free. I threw the clippers into the bushes, closed the patrol car back door. The intruder was standing in front of me, close enough to do me harm, both of us intermittent and ghoulish in the police flashers, like quantum cats.

"Sorry," I said, "my mistake. But please, think of

something better than breaking into people's houses. There's no future in that."

He had the forbearance, even at his young age, to not reply. He turned and loped off into the night, his good arm cradling his injured arm. The next time we saw him, that arm was in a proper cast.

I went back up to our porch, watched the policemen converge on the cars and discover that their suspect was gone. They argued among themselves, then turned to look up at us. We went inside. I put my hands on my wife's shoulders. "Please don't go," I said.

She looked at me, one eyebrow raised, the opposite eyelid lowered, as she did.

"Come with me," she said.

THE END

RIVER ROAD

We're being driven down River Road; it's getting narrower and narrower; tall tree trunks line up on both sides. The pavement gives way to gravel, then dirt. We trick them—and they do, they slow the car. We jump out, fall, roll, get up, run through a gap in the trees.

ACKNOWLEDGMENTS

Many thanks to the following.

Abbe Blum for her developmental editing of early versions of this novel.

Alison Galloway, Professor Emerita of Anthropology, University of California Santa Cruz, for her assistance with clarifying the science in the story. (Any remaining misrepresentations are my responsibility.)

Erika Goldman and the staff of Bellevue Literary Press for giving this book a chance and for guiding it to its best for publication.

Carolyn Kuebler, editor, *New England Review*, for her editing and publication of a short story of mine, for helping me to connect with Bellevue Literary Press, and for her new novel.

Margo Majewska, longtime partner, now my wife, for her ideas and support.

Jan van der Zwaag, shrink extraordinaire, for his encouragement and his help in reading my psyche.

Ania and Marcello, for allowing me to spend time in dog mind.

Bellevue Literary Press is devoted to publishing literary fiction and nonfiction at the intersection of the arts and sciences because we believe that science and the humanities are natural companions for understanding the human experience. We feature exceptional literature that explores the nature of consciousness, embodiment, and the underpinnings of the social contract. With each book we publish, our goal is to foster a rich, interdisciplinary dialogue that will forge new tools for thinking and engaging with the world.

To support our press and its mission, and for our full catalogue of published titles, please visit us at blpress.org.

Bellevue Literary Press
New York